LOST IN IBIZA

LOST IN IBIZA

REBECCA FRAYN

First published in 2024 by Rebecca Frayn,
in partnership with Whitefox Publishing

www.wearewhitefox.com

Copyright © Rebecca Frayn, 2024

ISBN 9781915635761
eBook ISBN 9781915635778
Audiobook ISBN 9781915635785

Rebecca Frayn asserts the moral right to be
identified as the author of this work.

While every effort has been made to trace the owners of
copyright material reproduced herein, the author would
like to apologise for any omissions and will be pleased to
incorporate missing acknowledgements in any future editions.

Cover artwork © Kate Bellm

Designed and typeset by Couper Street Type Co.
Cover design by Luke Bird
Author photo by David Loftus
Project management by Whitefox
Printed and bound by CPI Group (UK) Ltd, Croydon CRO 4YY

For Finn, Jack and Emmy.
Bone of my bone.
Flesh of my flesh.

1

Alice turned for the stairs, only to retreat again. But still she agonised, the minutes slipping away.

'Just tell me I'd be mad to go. That's all I need you to say.'

Franny was leaning against the open doorway of her flat, frowning at Alice in exasperation.

'In all honesty . . .' Franny held up her phone to show her the time. 'You've messed about so long, the chances of you making this flight are probably zero.'

In a flash of late resolve, Alice pulled her bag on to her back. She thought about going forward to offer a farewell kiss on the lips, but knowing it risked being mistaken as an olive branch, she only turned and ran. *You have nothing to fear but fear itself.* She ran down the stairs, and along the still-shuttered high street. She ran, dodging early morning commuters, stepping for a moment into the klaxon blare of an oncoming bus to circumvent them. She passed Mustafa unloading the first deliveries of the day.

'Hey! What's a crackalackin' girl?'

But she only raised her hand in salute and kept on running until she reached the underground station. And once the train released her at the other end, she resumed her run, weaving through the crowded airport terminal, arriving just moments before the gate closed.

Even as she took her seat on the plane, she kept an eye on the exit, holding its offer of release in reserve. Though it felt like the strangeness of her mission must be written all over her face, no one turns. Once the doors were secured and the plane airborne, she sat back and forced herself to focus on the view. She'd forgotten the luminosity of the sky when viewed from such a height. Forgotten too how the clouds resembled the kind of pillowy constructions a child might draw. Far below, the surface of the Earth was no more than a vast patchwork of green and brown, every now and then a snaking waterway traced in brilliant silver by the morning sun.

And then, much sooner than she had hoped, the plane was descending, passing low over a sea flecked and dimpled by the wind, and now an undulating coastline was rushing into view. She glimpsed a landscape that rose and fell in a series of wooded mountains and valleys. Moments later the plane was skating low over salt plains tinged an iridescent pink. As the wheels struck the tarmac, a great triumphal roar rose up from the stag party a few rows back, as if a marauding army were preparing to lay siege. Alerted by the buzz of signal returning to her phone, she glanced down to find the text message she had written still sitting, unsent.

Hey there! Change of plan! Decided to come after all!

For a second, her index finger hovered over send. But realising it was the very fact that no one was expecting her that gave her the courage to continue, she deleted the message instead.

Only moments earlier, William had paused at his study window to watch the relay of workers bring in tables and chairs for his birthday party. The song of turtle doves floated up from the trees, and the morning sun haloed the immaculate lawns and abundant flower beds of his handsome estate. The crystalline sunlight somehow lent the view the quality of a waking dream and he saw it all as if from a distance. Today he was half a century old. Somehow a measure of time he had always associated with history lessons had now attached itself to him.

For some while he had been disturbed by the distant roar of machinery rising from the forest that crowded along the garden's periphery. And now his caretaker came gliding into view, borne smoothly through the treetops on the hydraulic arm of a crane. As his chainsaw brought side branches crashing to the ground, the full sweep of the distant Mediterranean Sea, for so long half screened by trees, was appearing in a distant dazzle of blue. Cressida had evidently set the poor man the task of maximising their sea views in time for his birthday celebrations. *Dear God. Was there no end to the obsessive perfectionism of his wife's preparations?*

William took in the newly revealed views where sea now rose to marry imperceptibly with sky. And before he could prevent it, that forbidden possibility had crept crab-like to the forefront of his mind again: the blissful oblivion a man might find there in the fathomless depths of that ocean. A bottle of whisky for courage. The dark of night for cover. If the creatures of the sea didn't devour him first, his body might be found by fishermen washed up on the shores of Morocco.

He was too immersed in his reverie, too stroked by the solace of an exit plan, to note the far distant outline of Alice's plane as it passed along the blurred union where sea met sky, on its slow southwards descent to the airport.

She hoped the eGates might refuse to admit her. And when the automated gates only thudded open, she prayed instead that the customs officer might step in to halt her progress. *You're no longer the person documented here. Come back when you've worked out who you are.* But instead he only nodded her on and she found herself expelled into the Arrivals terminal, to join the boisterous crowds of disembarking passengers. Clubbers, new age hippies, crocodile chains of families on package holidays wheeling suitcases.

Since she had no money, she walked to the edge of the terminal and raised a thumb. One last throw of the dice. If no one stopped, she would just have to find a way to get home again. But she had no sooner raised her thumb than a pick-up truck had pulled to a halt with a young, dark-haired woman at the wheel. The woman emanated a febrile energy, her skin burnt such a deep shade by the sun that the whites of her eyes and teeth flashed startlingly bright, an Indian medallion shining in her nose, and silver bracelets encircling her mahogany arms.

'Amor!'

Even her bare toes each bore their own individual ring. Alice's spirits momentarily lifted as she took her in and she leant to offer her hand through the open window.

'Hey!'

'Where you headed?'

Alice had to squint against the dazzle of sunlight. 'Anywhere near . . .' – she checked the message on her phone – '. . . the Sant Vicent church?'

'Great. We're both headed north, then!' The woman leant over to throw open the door, smiling a warm welcome as Alice climbed in beside her. 'Let's get out of here. This place is the pits.'

The back of the pick-up truck was crammed with farming paraphernalia and the smell of something vegetal filled the small cabin. They passed a series of billboards promoting club nights – *What's Your Vice? A State of Trance, Reclaim the Dance Floor* – and the woman gestured towards them.

'You'll be a long way from all of this, you know.'

Alice nodded emphatically. 'Good!'

The woman gave her sidelong glance. A flash of that dis-arming smile again. 'So why Ibiza?'

'Oh.' Alice forced a laugh. 'Just some messed-up family stuff I have to deal with.'

The woman nodded, her glance shrewd and attentive, but Alice doesn't want to be drawn. 'What about you?'

She had come from Chile to work on one of the ecological farms that were springing up on the island, the woman told her. Alice turned to examine her more closely, taking in her gleaming face and the musky scent of vetiver that rose from her clothes. The woman laughed at Alice's surprise.

'Not what you were expecting, right? In the south they dance, but in the north we dig.'

'And then you dance.'

She laughed. 'Exactly.'

Very soon, the scrubby urbanisation had fallen away and there was nothing to be seen but farmland on either side, fields where sheep bent their heads to graze. After a little while, they passed through a village so small it was no more than a single street rising uphill; on one side a small supermarket, on the other a church, its solid plaster walls a blinding white against the blue of the sky. The lamp posts were strung with bunting and a team of men were toiling to construct a double line of bonfires in an open field beside the church. They were prepar-ing for the summer solstice celebrations, the woman explained.

The road rose more steeply out of town until they crested the summit, to discover a wide expanse of valley stretching away to the far distant glimmer of sea. Then they were swooping down the other side, the engine clattering and straining at each turn.

The pin he had sent her turned out to be little more than a hamlet. Apart from a whitewashed church, there was nothing but a deserted public tennis court and a community centre, closed for siesta. The woman stopped the van in front of the shuttered church, and looked about.

'Are you really sure about this?'

'I have never been less sure of anything in my entire life.' Alice tilted her sunglasses to look at the woman over the top. 'But I'm here now. Might as well get this done.' She stretched out her hand in farewell.

'Alice.'

'Paloma.'

'Wish me luck . . .'

'Buena suerte, amor! Until we meet again.'

As the pick-up took off, the woman turned to look back for a moment and, squinting in the sunlight, Alice gestured like a ballerina taking her final bow, one hand glissading all the way to the floor. But no sooner had the noise of the departing truck faded than the roar of cicadas rose up to fill the silence, and that fist had clenched within again.

A footpath wound away from the church passing almond groves on one side and dense forest on the other, just as his directions had described. But she found herself rooted to the spot. To proceed or turn back, that was the question. A car heading in the direction she had just come from sped towards her and she raised a hand to flag it down, before letting it fall again. Instead, she set off with renewed resolve along the dirt track that twisted away through the trees.

After a little while, she came to a boundary wall with a gate that had been propped open, and as she stepped through onto the gravelled drive, the wildness of the forest abruptly gave way to the clean lines of precisely manicured gardens, the stately palm trees in the distance revealing a lavishly scaled property.

Half screened by cypress trees, she thought she saw a glimmer of white walls and paused again, as the deafening dry rasp of cicadas moved through her. There would always be the before and the after. Then she stepped towards the house as if compelled by an invisible hand.

A row of agapanthus lined the drive in a blaze of blue, beyond them a wide expanse of lawn stacked with scores of tables and chairs. Drawing closer, the glimmer of white revealed itself to be the flank of a handsomely restored old farmhouse. Then a man emerged from a side door, gazing so intently at whatever he was reading on his phone that his slow steps soon came to a complete halt. His full head of hair and upright stance gave a youthful impression that was only countered, as she came abreast of him, by the lines about his eyes and the scattering of grey at his temples.

'Hi there . . .' Though she spoke softly, he looked up with a start, frowning first in puzzlement and then with a dawning amazement that slowly unlocked the hinge of his jaw as he took her in. Like someone in a dream, her feet kept walking her towards him until she came to an uncertain halt just a few feet away.

'Sorry to just burst in on you like this!' she heard herself say.

His mouth opened and closed, but no sound emerged. He tried again.

'Holy friggin' moley. I don't believe it. Alice . . . Is it really you?' She nodded, struggling to hold an approximation of a smile. 'Happy birthday.'

His mind was reeling as he blinked and blinked again at the sight of this smiling young woman with wild hair that framed a radiant face. The resemblance to her mother at the same age was so striking it seemed for a moment that Jess's ghost had appeared before him. Time running backwards. Death undone.

'My God . . .' The same exclamation rising again and again, unbidden to his lips. 'My God . . . So you decided to come after all!'

'The gate was open and I'm afraid I took it as an invitation to just mosey on in . . .'

The exact same spirited delivery Jess would have employed. As if in a trance, he moved forward with his hand extended in a formal greeting but found in his confusion that he had embraced her instead. She submitted with a certain formality, patting his back as if to steady him.

'When you said you couldn't come – what was it you said – that you *"didn't fly on principle"*, we just assumed it was a polite way of saying you weren't quite ready to meet us yet . . .' he began, stepping back to survey her again. 'And that was fine . . . No one could blame you for wanting to take things slowly.' He scratched the nape of his neck as he always did when under extreme duress. 'Christ.' He thought for a moment he might topple, the ability of his legs to hold him upright momentarily deserting him, as a peculiar sensation of liquidity passed through them.

'It's a bit mad, I know.' She grimaced.

He was trying hard to focus through the disorientation of colliding thoughts.

'And it's actually true that I don't fly on principle anymore. Only last night I got this email reminding me to check in and I suddenly thought – why not! Just this once.'

Though outwardly he was nodding, inwardly he was hastily rushing to piece the missing fragments together. He had sent her that flight. Of course he had. And in the rush of competing distractions completely forgotten to cancel it when she declined. He needed time to take this in. Time to think through all the likely consequences. To prepare his wife. But even in the midst of his panic he could also see that it was too late to do anything but ad lib. So he forced a rictus smile and made a supreme effort to rally.

'You must come and meet Cressida and the kids! They're going to be so thrilled you changed your mind. But I should warn you that the whole place is in uproar. Cressida's gone into full party mode. We're gearing up for this huge bloody birthday bash on Saturday. No idea what possessed me to agree . . . And now we're in the middle of this insane heatwave.' He turned towards the house, calling ahead. 'Cressida. Darling. You're never going to *believe* this!'

They passed through a grove of bent olive trees whose massive twisted trunks suggested the passage of centuries. Here and there the elegant column of a cypress tree drew the eye upwards to the canopy of blue. The wide flank of lawn was an improbable shade of emerald and as springy underfoot as a luxurious wool carpet. He dimly discerned it as if for the first time through her eyes. They entered under the shade of a long pergola, weighted with a vine on which grapes were swelling. At the kitchen door, he caught the scent of jasmine. William called out again, anxious to get the next bit done.

They stepped out of the sun-thickened air into the cool shade of a well-appointed yet artfully rustic kitchen filled with bustling activity. Mary, the Filipino housekeeper, was unpacking dozens of *shisha* pipes from sheets of bubble wrap, the glass bases and silver stems gleaming in the shadowed room.

'Darling. We have a surprise visitor!'

Cressida turned with a distracted air. 'Are you the Moroccan pouf person?'

'This is Alice! *Alice*, Alice . . .'

'Alice?' Cressida blinked as if she were receiving a series of internal electrical shocks, her voice when she retrieved it no more than a whisper. She was looking at Alice as if at a ghost.

'I invited her. Sent her a ticket. But when she said no, there seemed no point in telling you.'

'You *invited* her?'

She hung for a moment, suspended midway between social politeness and open incredulity. 'You *invited* her and didn't *tell* me?' Her gaze slid back to Alice, her eyes wide with shock.

'Oh, my God. Look at you. Oh, just look at you . . .' Her hand had flown first to her heart and then her mouth, looking between Alice and William and back again in disbelief. 'Of course it's you . . . What an amazing thing. You have her face. Her smile.'

The two women stood wordlessly scrutinising one another, and just as William was about to try and rescue them, Cressida located her social self and stumbled forward to offer a perfunctory hug.

'Well, how wonderful. What a treat! What a surprise! But you're going to have to bear with us, I'm afraid. Everything is so topsy-turvy – we have a house jam-packed with guests.'

Alice started to explain all over again about the spontaneity of her decision but waving a dismissive hand, Cressida had already begun talking over her, issuing instructions to Mary about giving her one of the children's bedrooms. Though Alice tried to insist she didn't want to disrupt anything, Cressida was already hurrying to the door, distracted by the noise of a delivery truck that had begun backing into the courtyard.

'Oh, for goodness' sake . . . excuse me for one minute, will you . . . It's the Bedouin tent people and I'm just going to have to . . .'

The truck juddered to a halt in front of the house and a retinue of perspiring workers jumped down and began to unload the long rolled sections of canvas.

'No, no, not there, not there!' Cressida rushed out into the bright sunshine and disappeared from view, though the indignation of her querulous tone was still distantly audible. 'Dios mío. Poned sentido común!'

There was a sound of running feet on the polished cement floor and two sun-kissed children burst into the room. They came to an abrupt halt at the sight of Alice, and William placed a hand on each of their shoulders to mark the solemnity of the moment. He swallowed. 'Alice. I'd like to introduce you to Lola and Joe.'

'Hey Lola. Hi Joe.' Alice bent to shake Lola's hand but Joe thrust his hand behind his back before burying his face in his father's leg.

'Lola is seven – and Joe – tell Alice how old you are . . .'

'Four and three quarters,' Joe offered emphatically, though he made no attempt to uncover his face.

'Look. Found something you might like.' Alice took out a papery snakeskin she had found on the path and let it slowly unravel to reveal its impressive length. She held it out to him. But though he risked a quick glance, he couldn't quite bring himself to take it, watching with covetous eyes as Lola accepted it instead, and ran a proprietorial finger along its papery length.

'I would have told them all about you when your email came. I figured they were probably old enough now. But Cressida wasn't so sure.' William looked down to address the children. 'So. guys. I have quite a story for you. There was once a little girl called Alice, who was brought up by her father after her mother died. Only one day, when she was twenty-one, this man she had always thought was her father sat her down and told her he had a secret. That though he loved her very much, he wasn't actually her *real* father after all.' William kept glancing between the children and Alice, trying to gauge the effect of his words on both parties. 'And can you guess who her real family turned out to be?'

'Was it us?' the little girl said in a whisper, her grave eyes fixed on her father.

'That's right, Lola. It was us. And now here she is. Alice is your big sister and she has come all the way from England to meet us!'

The eyes of both children pivoted from their father, to rest with solemnity on Alice again. 'Is you true life?' Joe asked, finally stepping from behind his father's leg to examine her with undisguised suspicion.

'I certainly hope so!'

She undoubtedly gave every impression of being real,

William thought, his eyes riveted upon her. *His daughter. His adult daughter. A flesh and blood entity! Here under his very roof.* Appearing to sense his scrutiny, Alice turned to meet his gaze with a quizzical expression.

He gestured with palms open to the sky. 'I'm afraid I'm still too gobsmacked to quite take this all in . . .'

'I feel bad now,' she said. 'Just descending on you so unexpectedly like this.'

'Don't be ridiculous – we couldn't be more delighted . . . It's just going to take a bit of time to properly sink in, that's all. And you'll have to be patient with us while it does. I mean, never in my wildest dreams had I expected a fiftieth birthday present of quite this magnitude!'

A choked sensation of something that heralded tears compressed his throat and he turned in confusion to his children for rescue. 'Why don't we show Alice around while Mary gets Lola's bedroom sorted out for her?' His phone emitted a small bleep and he looked blankly at it before recalling its significance with a vexed shake of the head. He was scheduled to take a conference call in ten minutes, he explained to Alice apologetically. Too late to rearrange now. Amidst all the party mayhem, it was still a working day for him. But he just had time to give her a quick tour.

With the children trailing at their heels, they stepped into a high-ceilinged room where an elegant arrangement of contemporary furniture was set out on a gleaming floor. A vast picture window gave onto the luxuriant gardens, and beyond them distant views of sea and forest. Three guests lay napping on sunloungers, small piles of suntan lotion and books scattered about them. At the far end of the lawn, the team of workers had begun to lay down the long flanks of canvas, while Cressida paced out the footings and one of the men bent to make marks with a spray can.

The original farmhouse had been a ruin when they first came across it, William explained as they strolled. No power, no water. And despite being overseen by a fashionable Belgian architect, the project had proved a nightmare. Licences that took years. Byzantine regulations that had to be sidestepped with cunning ingenuity. As he talked, he threw open different doors to reveal a series of immaculate bedrooms, then a well-equipped gym and an air-conditioned wine store with bottles stacked from floor to ceiling in order of grape and vintage. He paused for a moment at the door to one of the bedrooms, experiencing an unfamiliar satisfaction at how well everything looked as sunshine slanted sideways through the windows, forming a golden aura about the cut flowers on the side table.

In the garden, they passed a series of newly renovated outhouses. The first had been converted into a games room, and he pointed out the sturdy wooden wine press they had retained in one corner. They had taken great care to retain as many of the original features as possible, he explained. William moved on to the cinema room. 'This used to be the pig pen and so we wanted to preserve a rustic simplicity,' he said, tucking a trailing light cable out of sight beneath one of the vintage Moroccan rugs.

They emerged into the sunlight again, skirting three Filipino gardeners who were crouched in the beds, deadheading the flowers.

'And now – here we are. Living the dream!' His tone was lightly self-satirising. 'We feel like proper locals.'

'How's your Spanish?' she asked.

'Absolutely atrocious, I'm sorry to say.'

The sceptical expression that fleeted across her face at this was so precisely her mother's, he was floored all over again. Jess, of course, would have teased him mercilessly about the whole enterprise.

'You've relocated to Ibiza?' He could hear her mocking upward inflexion. 'Well, guess you always were a man of hidden shallows!'

His phone began to ring in his hand. This would be his conference call coming through, he said in an apologetic tone. She must excuse him. He'd try to wind it up as soon as he could. He made an expansive gesture as if offering her everything she surveyed, while the phone continued to clamour in his hand.

'Look, make yourself at home, will you. Our caretaker will show you to your room and dinner will be at eight. I shall very much look forward to talking further. We have a whole lifetime to catch up on! Where on earth will we start? And once we've started, how on earth will we ever stop?'

Mary stood observing this tableau of sir and the young woman from afar. Her head was a whirl of tasks to be attended to and her tray was growing heavy, the ice in the jug already melting. But she took care to stand like someone with all the time in the world, a half-smile at her lips. It was only the children's visible unease now their father had gone that gave her the courage to come forward. She set her tray down on a nearby table and dipped her head as she offered the visitor a glass of chilled hibiscus tea, keeping her eyes on the ground.

'Thank you.' Alice acknowledged receipt of the drink with a smile that Mary was at pains not to receive.

'My name's Alice,' she said, extending her hand, and though Mary knew she had no choice but to reciprocate, she did so with a shrinking reluctance.

This was a difficulty that fortunately arose only very rarely, the guest whose overfriendliness inadvertently breached the convention of Mary's invisibility. Fortunately, her years of domestic service had taught her how to shake off even the most persistent of kind intentions. She usually began by responding as monosyllabically as courtesy allowed, and if that didn't work and the attempt at conversation persisted, she would take refuge in such jumbled English, her interlocutor had no choice but to release her with a puzzled smile.

'And you are?' Alice pressed.

More recently, Mary had evolved a new strategy and her eyes slid sideways to call on Lola, who, readily understanding what was required of her, spoke up in a prim voice. 'Her name is Mary and she looks after us and cleans stuff.'

Mary had dropped her eyes to the floor again, offering only the smallest inclination of assent, before stepping back with relief as Rene arrived to offer his hand to Alice in his characteristically forthright fashion. He was the caretaker, he told Alice, and also Mary's husband. He had come at Cressida's request to show Alice to her room, which was now ready.

'So you're both from the Philippines, then?' Alice said, scrutinising first one and then the other. Mary looked at Rene, who only nodded. But Alice was not to be so readily deflected. It was as if the more they attempted to evade her, the more compelled she became to engage them.

'Do you have children?' she asked. Again Rene nodded. 'A daughter. Eight years old.'

'And she lives here?'

'With Mary's mother. In the Philippines.' His tone had a flat matter-of-factness.

Alice threw a compassionate glance at Mary. But having no desire to receive a stranger's unsolicited sympathy, Mary made a great ceremony of gathering up the empty glasses and restoring order. Alice was about to come forward to help, but was distracted instead by the sight of Rene picking up her backpack.

'No, no – please,' Alice said hurrying forward to try and forestall him. 'There's really no need to do that. Let me . . .'

For a moment, they tussled, Alice holding fast to one strap while Rene grasped the other, their smiles crossing like swords. But despite his deference, it was apparent he hadn't the slightest intention of allowing this unwelcome challenge to the hierarchy of the household. So, after a brief stand-off, Alice released the bag to him, muttering her effusive thanks as she followed on behind. Mary picked up the tray, calling for the children to accompany her, stepping back with relief into the anonymity of her appointed role.

All afternoon the preparations for the party continued. There were workers still constructing the tent, while another team set up a bar area. As Cressida walked about, making a careful inspection, she was pleased to see that Rene had trimmed the rounded balls of westringia into such perfect spheres that even when she examined them from different angles, she could find no fault in the solidity of their neat outlines.

She came to a standstill at the corner of the house, listening to the hiss of the shower running in Lola's bathroom, the shock of Alice's unexpected arrival rushing upon her all over again. William's daughter was here. William's long-lost daughter had come. Her husband had invited Alice to his party without even bothering to run the idea past her first. And now, as if she didn't have enough to contend with already, the whole sorry saga was going to have to be played out under the fascinated scrutiny of their guests. Well. No time like the present.

On an inward breath let. On the outward breath go.

She strode down to the pool and surveyed the scene. A number of guests were dozing in the blistering afternoon sun, while others chatted or read, and she came to an uncertain halt before them. Some were old friends, others extended family members, and they had been arriving on flights in groups of twos and fours for the past few days, most inclined to do little once they had unpacked but bask beside the pool like furless seals.

'Ladies and gentlemen. Just to let you know. The Formentera boat trip will be departing at crack of dawn tomorrow,' Cressida declared, in a jolly mock travel rep voice, and there were muffled cries of polite anticipation from behind the sunglasses and Kindles. 'I'm afraid William and I will be too tied up here to join you. But rest assured that everything has been taken care of. I'll email everyone an updated schedule.'

'Ah cheers, Cress.' Marcus, an old banking colleague of William's, rested his Kindle on his chest. 'No rest for the hostess with the mostest, hey!'

She turned away to watch William's cousin, Charlie, doing lengths of the pool as the general conversation resumed again, trying to steady herself by studying the controlled precision of his stroke. Seeing that she was poised to say more, he swam to the edge of the pool, yanking off his goggles, as if to hear her better. And knowing she must seize the moment, she cleared her throat.

'Oh. And I'd better warn you all. While I have you in one place. A rather extraordinary thing has just happened.' What words would come next, she wondered.

Charlie trumpeted water from his nose, before squinting expectantly up at her. 'Go on, then. We're all ears . . . '

'Well, we had a bit of a shock a few months ago when William found out that unbeknownst to him, he had fathered a daughter, who was now twenty-one.'

'What? William has an illegitimate child! Bloody hell, Cress.'

Cressida nodded, aware of a deepening hush as even those who had been only half attending caught the air of suppressed agitation and turned to offer their full attention.

'Her name is Alice . . .' If she could only maintain this jaunty confiding tone, she saw a way she might just get through this. 'And you're never going to believe it, but . . .'

Every screen and page had by now been lowered, all eyes resting so intently upon her that, despite her nerves, she felt the little leap of gratification every storyteller experiences when they sense their audience in the palm of their hand.

'But Alice has just turned up here! We had absolutely no idea she was coming. We've both just met her for the very first time!'

The exclamations of amazement and incredulity were so heartfelt her tear ducts burnt and welled with a fiery wash of self-pity. Marcus emitted a low whistle of wonder.

'No way!'

'HERE?'

'What. Literally just now?'

'Not literally just now, surely . . .?'

The row of expectant faces waited agog to hear more. She sat down on the edge of the pool, the soothing cool of the water about her calves somewhat reviving her. 'Yes. Literally. About an hour ago.' She gazed down at her feet fractured by the water, trying to take in this strange turn of events.

'Fucking hell, Cress!'

Now she had said it out loud, the improbability of the whole thing had settled into a more factual event that must be dealt with. 'So you'll all get a chance to meet her at dinner tonight.' She got to her feet again, brushing down her dress with a businesslike gesture.

'That's completely mental!' Charlie's abundance of curly chest hair made her think with fleeting discomfort of a Labradoodle. He shot her a penetrating glance before propping his forearms on the warm lip of the pool. 'You OK, Cress? You're white as a sheet.'

To her dismay, she found she could no longer trust herself to speak. Nothing quite like sympathy to dismantle one's front of house.

'Oh, I'll live . . .' she managed. 'Never a dull moment when you're married to William, that's for sure.'

There was a hush as she turned and walked away with a poker-straight back towards the house, soon followed, as she had expected, by a rush of urgent and exhilarated conferring once they judged she had moved out of earshot.

Alice walked about Lola's room taking in the quantity of toys that lined the shelves in neat rows. Then, feeling drained to the core, she lay down on the little bed. In rapid succession, she had just met her biological father, his wife who, she supposed, she must try to look on as a stepmother, and after all these years of being an only child, two younger half-siblings. The accumulation of encounters had come so hard and fast, each was freighted with a dreamlike unreality.

What am I to this man? What is he to me?

She lay back and watched the ceiling fan as it spun, becoming aware of the most curious sensation of weightlessness: as if she had slipped out of her own skin, and her very identity was being dispersed by the movement of air. Welling tears blurred the turning blades.

'He hadn't even told his kids about me . . .'

From the garden, the steady beat of a mallet striking wood evoked an irresistible torpor. The turtle doves were calling from the trees, while closer at hand, someone was conducting a hissed *sotto voce* conversation. In her half-conscious state, it took a while to realise, as snatches reached her through the open door, that it must be William and Cressida.

'Everyone looked pretty stunned, I can tell you . . .' Cressida was saying in a querulous tone. William's low, more reasoned response was lost to Alice. But fragments of Cressida's indignation continued to reach her.

'*You* need a bit of time to get your head round this? My God, William. What about *me*? What about the poor *children*?' Followed by a dainty trumpeting noise of someone blowing into a handkerchief. A fly was thrumming against the glass pane of the window, a drowsy hot summer sound somehow imbued with a subtle command to sleep. And within moments Alice had succumbed.

It was the furtive giggling and whispering of the children at Alice's bedroom door a little while later that made Mary hasten to investigate. She had only to peer over their heads through the half-open door to see the cause: Alice lying fast asleep on the bed, curled on her side, the towel that had been wrapped about her now fallen open to reveal the curve of one breast. Mary had to stifle her cry of consternation as she rushed forward to shoo the children away and, now she was in the room, found herself compelled to restore Alice's modesty by drawing the towel over her. Then, tiptoeing about the room with the lightness of foot that had become second nature to her, continued, out of sheer force of habit, to gather up the discarded clothes Alice had dropped on the floor, before unpacking her backpack, puzzled at how little the girl had brought with her. She put the single T-shirt and shorts away in the cupboard, where they looked more like scanty items mistakenly left by a previous guest.

At the bottom of Alice's backpack she found two books, together with her passport. Mary looked at the pictures on the book covers, but since she couldn't read English, the words printed there were no more than clusters of markings. A folded piece of paper, lodged for safekeeping between the pages of one of them, fluttered sideways. It was typed and had the appearance of an official letter – the kind she had to ask Rene to read out loud to her – on its masthead a lion and a horse rearing up on either side of a shield and crown. Exactly the same grand coat of arms she was accustomed to seeing on the cover of the family's British passports. She put the letter back where she had found it and set the books on the bedside table, all the while stealing little glances at Alice as she slept.

Who would have dreamt sir had a long-lost adult daughter who would just show up one sunny afternoon like this? Cressida had briefly filled her in, and already Mary was relishing the prospect of sharing the news at church on Sunday. The stories that revealed the fathomless moral foibles of the wealthy *banyaga* employers were always the most highly prized and widely disseminated.

Before leaving, Mary bowed her head over Alice and muttered a few quiet words of mitigation for a child born out of wedlock – *O Lord, Jesus Christ, Redeemer and Saviour, if you will forgive our transgressions, I promise to give You praise and glory in love and in service all the days of my life* – before withdrawing with only the barest disturbance of air molecules.

Of all the most outlandish things . . . His daughter . . . A young woman of twenty-one. Arriving out of the blue like that. William had barely focused on the interminable conference call, and now stood once more at the window of his study, ruminatively twisting his wedding ring as he observed the perspiring workers carrying kilims into the completed Moroccan tent.

He attempts to gather himself in readiness for this very public encounter that is about to unfold. The impression that Jess had returned from the grave had shaken him to the very core. It was both incongruous and yet reassuring that the party preparations should continue as if nothing of any great significance had occurred. All afternoon more delivery vans had roared and bumped their way up the drive. Then four new guests, fresh from the airport, with Rene dragging their suitcases a few steps behind, and Cressida, like a solicitous maître d', at their helm.

He began to pace the room. When Alice had declined his invitation some months ago with the puzzling rationale of not flying on principle, he had, though he could never admit it, been as much relieved as crestfallen, for the news of a now adult child from his past had not gone down well with Cressida. She had been adamant they tell no one, not even the children. And clearly, if Alice wasn't yet ready for a face-to-face encounter, there wasn't much more he could do. At least for the time being. So, he had drafted an upbeat email in response, proposing that they might perhaps meet instead for a cup of coffee when he was next in the UK. But finding it impossible to decide whether he was really ready for such an encounter, the email had remained in his drafts folder ever since. And then there she was, the next move wrested from his hands, just strolling towards him across the lawn. Why on earth had she not sent a text to warn him of her change of heart? But hadn't so much of his own twenties involved rushing headlong into things with reckless disregard for the consequences? Indeed, Cressida would doubtless say that Alice was the living embodiment of his youthful impetuosity. And now this living embodiment has taken up residence in the very bosom of his family and friends without any of the emotional or practical preparation that would have preceded her arrival had he only known she was on her way.

William slid his hand behind one of the rows of books that lined the far wall and brought out the bottle of Scotch he had been resisting all day. *Drink this artisanal whisky any way you like*, its label declared in a breezy fashion, *there are no rules that can't be broken.* He went to the mini fridge, but the ice box was empty. Would it be pushing his luck to try to get more from the kitchen without risking coming face to face with her? Knowing perfectly well it was a failure of will and as such to be regretted, he poured himself a generous measure and gulped it down anyway. For how often did a man turn fifty *and* meet his long-lost daughter all in the same week? The merit of this rationale struck him as so compelling it led very naturally to a modest top-up, which was so effective it was at once apparent that another measure would be advisable. A long-closed door onto a past life had sprung open. The abstract writer of that startling email had been superseded by the beguiling physical reality of this radiant young woman. A young woman who would doubtless have questions. Questions that were going to require extremely delicate handling . . .

He returned to the window and watched as Rene struggled across the lawn, bowed under the weight of the large sack he carried over one shoulder. Arriving at the edge of the pool, he slit open the bag, before upending its contents into the water. William sipped his whisky and watched while Rene returned several times more, bent low beneath the weight of a new sack, while the guests on the nearby sunloungers read their books, oblivious to his toil. Only Marcus, raising himself on one elbow, observed Rene, before flopping down again with a yawn, as if the very sight of so much exertion had sapped his last ounce of strength.

Could he actually hold it together for the next two days, he wondered? He set to work straightening the spines of the books. In the moment of aligning, there was a fleeting stillness at his core – as if someone had switched off the tremble of agitation that incessantly vibrated like the engine of a boat. And the inevitability of the agitation's imminent return when he was done only sweetened and deepened the beauty of the passing stillness. Very soon the books were aligned in one single straight-spined entity from A to Z.

He paced about the room, finding himself in front of the painting he had been sweet-talked into purchasing by that silver-tongued art dealer. He had come across it in an elegant gallery on Cork Street one day, something about the burnish of the museum-class company in which it hung lending it an aura, not to mention a price tag, so compelling he had felt quite light-headed as he submitted his credit card. But the picture had no sooner been liberated from its elaborate export packaging than Cressida had declared it the ugliest thing she'd ever set eyes on, and consigned it to his study. He had come to see it as a barometer of his moods, since different lights and varying frames of mind made it strike him in such entirely contrasting ways. Sometimes – today – it appeared to be a lumpen assembly of paint, crudely applied, its brutalism mocking him at his naivety in ever having fallen for the dealer's hyperbole. But every now and then his eye would fall upon it and he would be startled to find it unexpectedly imbued with a subtle profundity.

Of late, his increasingly troubled investments had been much on his mind and now new anxieties crowded in to compound the old ones. After Alice's first email, Cressida had made a number of waspish allusions to the fact that Alice would doubtless want to stake some kind of legal claim on his estate. And there was no ducking the practical ramifications that would have to be ironed out now. Deals that would have to be struck. Moral if not legal obligations to be honoured. His best strategy by far would be to try and hold Alice off until after the party. The party was the thing. Though – something in his gut twisted and shrank – he would of course now have to include her in his speech.

He was just reaching for the whisky bottle again when a knock at the door made him jump, and opening it he found Rene waiting in the now darkening corridor. Their caretaker was a small wiry counterpart to his small wiry wife, though in contrast to her meek demeanour, his smiling deference was countered by an impression of a natural authority, discreetly subdued. William often found himself a little unnerved by the flashes of sublimated intelligence he glimpsed in him. Rene had a quickness of mind and an impressive pragmatism. There was no denying that if he were ever to leave, the entire household would soon grind to a halt. What a puzzle it must seem to the Renes of the developing world to have to serve the clod-footed fools the developed world saw fit to so handsomely remunerate. *Come the revolution, he'd have my guts for garters.* A queasy recollection came to him of all those folders filled by Rene with each month's bills and receipts, their punctilious frugality a chastening reproach to his own casual profligacy.

He knew of old that Rene's troubled expression could only herald a report about some new domestic setback. An unseasonal storm now forecast to break on Saturday. Or a blockage in the septic tank that meant the festivities would have to be conducted with a pungent whiff of raw sewage in the air. He waited. They had barely embarked on this long-planned weekend of fun and frivolity and already it appeared to be unravelling.

'Bad news, sir,' Rene said with a frown. 'We have problem with the pool.'

Though it had been pleasing to glimpse something of its seductive charms through the eyes of a newcomer, the truth was that beneath its well-appointed veneer, the house and gardens often felt like an assault course of ever evolving logistical headaches. Logistical headaches that William was entirely reliant on Rene to resolve. In a bid to remedy this uncomfortable dependency, he had recently made a concerted attempt to grasp the idiosyncratic foibles of saline pool maintenance. Yet somehow not a single technical detail had lodged in his brain.

And now, despite the brief intermission afforded by the whisky, a feeling of impending doom was settling upon William again. That cliché about carrying the weight of the world on one's shoulders turned out not to be a cliché at all. He felt stooped beneath his troubles. Two hundred guests about to gather in this sweltering heat without the possibility of a pool to refresh them. A long-lost daughter trailing history far better left to lie.

'I will leave it with you. But just remember we only have two days to get it sorted.' William was already hastening away down the corridor, jabbing a finger skywards as he went. 'Two days, Rene! Please let me know how you get on.'

At dinner on the terrace that night, William raised a toast to Alice, and the assembled guests followed suit, as their avid eyes feasted on this rare and thrilling spectacle of a father and daughter so new in their acquaintance. She felt the scorch of their curiosity. There were at least eighteen people present, mostly house guests, though a few were apparently friends who lived on the island – and an intriguing diversity of nationalities were represented in varying shades of lightly accented English. The elevating and pin-sharp light from the stars above their heads was countered by the earthbound silhouettes of the sturdy palm trees that grew all about the terrace, together with the comforting abundance laid out before them. At William's insistence, Alice found herself sitting at the head of the table, observing him hold forth with great animation, often glancing in her direction as if the evening was a performance entirely for her benefit.

The impression was heightened by the fizz of suppressed excitement in the air. She sensed that each guest was poised with questions they dared not voice quite yet. Instead, someone had brought up Quebec's recent banning of the niqab and burka.

'What if we ask any man who objects to a woman being uncovered to wear a blindfold?'

Alice tipped her head, offering an impish smile as she surveyed the uneasy expressions of her audience, some of whom appeared to fear the conversation was straying into contentious territory. She looked at Cressida, inviting her to respond, but Cressida only sat stiff-backed, every now and then brushing her hair from her face in a self-soothing gesture that was as unconscious as it was compulsive.

When Mary came to offer a platter of grilled fish, Alice politely declined, explaining she was vegan. That she was more than happy with just the vegetables.

'Oh no,' Cressida's face had fallen in dismay. 'I wish you'd said. The chef would have made something specially.'

Alice saw William examine first her and then the glassy-eyed *dorada* on his plate with a puzzled frown before taking up the bottle of wine, and leaning forward to pour her some, as if in compensation. She shook her head again, offering an apologetic smile. 'I hate to say this but I don't drink either.'

'Teetotal as well as vegan. My God. Are you in training to be a nun or something?'

She was accustomed to the covert defensiveness of the older generation whenever the topic of her veganism arose. How it seemed to trigger an assumption that she probably considered herself on a higher moral plane and would judge them accordingly. And perhaps, in truth, she did. Certainly, their facility for burying their heads in the sand often confounded her. William watched Mary slide only the vegetables onto her plate before filling his wine glass to the brim, apparently appropriating the portion Alice had spurned, and setting the bottle down with a small clunk as if to affirm his own moral certainty on these issues. Then he gulped down a mouthful of social lubricant before spooning a helping of dead animal into his mouth. *I tolerate all foibles at my table*, his smile strained to imply.

'And so father and daughter met for the first time this afternoon!' Unable to contain her curiosity any longer, Kate, who was seated midway between them, was glancing from Alice to William and back again, the bright sparkle of rings on her fingers illuminated by the candlelight, and duplicated by the gleam of enthralment in her eyes.

'Yes,' Alice nodded in unison with William, conscious of Cressida drawing herself more upright still, as if assuming a hawk-like vigilance.

'I'm still reeling, as you can imagine,' William said. 'Have to keep pinching myself!'

In the shadows of the doorway, Alice caught a momentary glimpse of Lola standing in her nightdress, her eyes like burning coals upon her, before Mary hurried forward to usher her upstairs again.

Cressida cleared her throat. 'Darling. Perhaps you should explain. It's not like you reneged on your parental duties or anything. Basically, twenty-one years ago, you and Alice's mother had the briefest of flings, didn't you? Just a one-night stand kind of thing. And then off you blithely went, completely oblivious that something so momentous had occurred! And for reasons we can only speculate on now, Alice's mother decided to keep the news to herself.' She took a deep breath, and when William still didn't prove forthcoming, pressed gamely on. 'You and I happened to get together shortly afterwards, didn't we? Didn't we darling? It must literally have been only about a month or two later. Do you remember?'

The charge of fascination in the air was as tangible as the metallic scent that heralds a summer storm, and the assembled guests turned to contemplate William's gnomic expression, compelled as much by what was being said as by the way in which the words appeared to skate across a hidden complexity they could only dimly discern.

'My God! How extraordinary!' an Italian who had been introduced as Giancarlo exclaimed, turning to address William. 'And so, for twenty-one years, you and Cressida had no idea Alice even existed!' Giancarlo waited for a response, but William was all at once so immersed in the delicate business of deboning his fish he didn't appear to hear him. So yet again, Cressida hastened to fill his silence.

'Not the slightest clue! Until Alice's email. Just a few months ago. Can you imagine? We were dumbfounded! Utterly dumbfounded . . .' She glanced at Alice with an expression of reproach.

Giancarlo addressed Alice. 'And you? Did you grow up knowing about William?'

'Not the foggiest idea. Until my father decided to tell me a few months ago. At least . . . well . . .' She cleared her throat, uttering a forced little laugh. 'I mean the man I had always *thought* was my father . . .' A silence elapsed. 'It was a bit of a bombshell for sure. Guess I'm still trying to process it.'

Giancarlo kept looking between them, nodding. 'How remarkable!' he said in wonderment. 'How privileged we are to witness this moment.'

Alice threw a quick appraising glance at William. 'The other strange part of it all is that according to my Dad . . . I was actually conceived on this island.'

An almost subliminal jolt of horror seemed to move through William as if something had fallen amongst the plates and cutlery with a great crash. He appeared to be struggling to maintain his composure as he surveyed the row of attentive faces, time suspended as everyone intently awaited his reply. Though Alice was at pains not to look in Cressida's direction, she couldn't help but form a dim impression of how very pallid she had grown in the half-light.

'Goodness! That's what he told you, did he?' He laughed, raising his palms to the sky in a *where do I start* kind of way.

'Well, to be quite honest with you, it's a long story. And now is probably not the best time to unpack its undoubted complexities!'

'Gosh!' Kate exclaimed, nodding her head several times with a bright encouraging smile, her eyes darting between the key protagonists. 'Isn't this all just completely riveting! And now here the two of you are, not only meeting for the first time, but on the very island where the whole story began . . .' She looked like she was readying herself to risk a new question, but paused with parted lips to glance uncertainly at William, whose glazed smile she appeared to read as tacit permission to proceed. 'And where, if you don't mind my asking, is your mama now?'

'Sadly, my mother died when I was still very young. So, I was raised by my father.' This time, through sheer force of habit, Alice didn't hesitate to use the possessive noun.

'And where did your mother originally come from . . . ?'

'The UK . . .' Alice understood the reason for Kate's puzzlement, and softening, decided to give her the explanation she was seeking. 'My grandfather was a Nigerian academic who came to the UK on a scholarship, where – to the disappointment of both sets of parents – he met my grandmother, who was from Tooting.'

'Gosh,' Kate said again, in a mesmerised tone, glancing now at Cressida to gauge whether too many eggshells were cracking underfoot. And noting Cressida's ashen countenance, she dabbed at the corners of her mouth with her napkin as if to impose a silence on herself. Casting her fixed smile upon Kate with silent gratitude, Cressida looked around the circle of faces, appearing to implore someone to steer them into safer waters. At which William threw open his arms, evidently equally eager to move things on.

'And now – my goodness – look at you, Alice – here you are all these years on – a young woman. Old enough in fact to be reading English at Cambridge . . .'

'Actually, I dropped out. Just a few weeks after I first emailed you.'

'Dropped out?' He looked crestfallen, as he took in that the trump card he had been saving to share with his guests was now valueless.

Despite her best efforts at restraint, Kate couldn't prevent herself from darting in again while he digested this. 'And what are you doing instead?'

'A bit complicated to explain. Environmental activism, mainly. I'm part of this group who are taking to the streets to . . .'

'Oh, my God. You're one of those hot-headed youth brigades who brought London to its knees!' Charlie, who had just taken a large sip of wine, gulped it down in his rush to release a great guffaw, slapping the table with the palm of his hand. 'Of course you are! That's magnificent.'

'So it was your lot who closed all the bridges!' William said, his tone poised between lightness and censure. 'All those attention-seeking stunts inconvenienced a lot of people, I can tell you. I happened to be in London at the time and it was an absolute bloody nightmare.'

'Oops . . . the gloves are off now,' Charlie ventured, *sotto voce*, to his neighbour.

Alice shrugged, holding her smile. 'Well. When your home's burning, I should have thought you'd value the fire alarm that alerts you . . .' She bit her lip, making a quick sweep of faces, surreptitiously observing her fellow guests as they picked at the diminishing sea life heaped with such abundance on their plates. There was so much she wanted to say that she wasn't sure she could swallow the words. For a brief moment she hovered midway between pursuing the issue or retreating. The moment hung suspended, before she clamped her hands beneath her thighs and pursed her lips. She looked about, conscious of a palpable relief as they observed her retreat. She wasn't about to denounce them after all. No need to mount a half-baked defence of their lifestyles. They were off the hook.

'*Touché!*' Kate raised her glass and downed it in one. 'Quite right, Alice. Well said you. It's all those takeaway coffee cups that make me so cross. And plastic straws. Just don't get me started on plastic straws.'

'I suppose you know that your newly discovered father is an ex-hedge fund manager who now dabbles in property development?' Giancarlo offered, as if compelled to make a full disclosure on his friend's behalf. Alice hoped her face remained impassive.

'Of course. First thing I did was check him out on Google.'

Cressida cleared her throat and looked around. 'More wine anyone?'

'Perhaps you should confess your latest piece of audacity, Will?' Charlie's leg had begun to jiggle as if a jubilant malice were pumping through his system. 'The sly old fox has just bagged one hundred and fifty thousand square metres of prime real estate, plus a licence to build on one of the most stunning bits of virgin coastline in the south! And there's meant to be a strict planning embargo on this island. No idea how he does it.'

'Oh, don't take any notice of Charlie, for goodness' sake,' William said, shifting under the burn of Alice's inspection, glancing at how her hands toyed with her water glass. 'I take environmental issues quite as seriously as the next person.' William turned to beam at everyone with a patient forbearance. 'We are moving with the times, I assure you. These days we're all about sustainability, renewable resources, energy efficiency and low-impact materials.'

'Don't that group of yours ask all their supporters to be ready and willing to be arrested?' Charlie asked Alice.

'Yup. If necessary. Sure.' She looked about the table, offering her most inclusive smile in an attempt to disarm. 'You all read the papers. You know what the scientists are saying. Please. Come and join us. We'd love to have you . . .'

William was beaming too as he looked about the table, as if inviting his guests to marvel at this wondrous creature he had produced. 'It's not easy being "woke", you know. Did you know she usually refuses to fly on principle?' He turned to Alice for confirmation. 'Isn't that true?'

She couldn't but take offence at the forced jocularity of his use of 'woke' and the hint of satirical inflexion with which he infused it. Suspecting he was directing his guests to be tolerant of her youthful idealism, an angry riposte rose to her lips. How tenaciously the one-percenters clung to their moral myopia. But once again, with a great effort of will, she only nodded. 'I do.'

'Given how much I have to travel, you will appreciate that I squirmed a little when I heard that! But despite declining my invitation to come to Ibiza because of it, Alice decided to make a last-minute exception – and now I understand better what a tussle with her conscience that was, I feel most honoured. What's that phrase you used . . .'

'Train not plane?'

'*Train not plane.* Exactly! Isn't that wonderful! And I want you to know that I will be giving the concept some serious consideration when I'm next planning my travel itinerary!' William sat back in his chair with expansive bonhomie. 'I must say, I'm beginning to think there's something to be said for a system of child-rearing in which you skip all the tantrums and cut straight to meeting as civilised adults. I mean, here we are engaging right from the get-go in some of the hot topics of the day!'

Cressida was contemplating them both with a perturbed

frown, while Kate remained so spellbound, her knife and fork hovered above her almost untouched plate. Charlie meanwhile was chewing his food like cud as he cogitated on this potent spectacle of a father and daughter still only hours old in their acquaintance. *The wonderful ironies of life!*, the mischievous light in his eye seemed to say. He smiled at Cressida to see how she was bearing up and she did her best to respond in kind, though the corners of her mouth barely lifted.

'It's going to be fascinating filling in the gaps, I must say,' William was telling the table at large. 'You'll have to be patient with us in the coming days. We have a lot of ground to cover.'

The finality of William's tone made it clear the subject was – for the time being – now closed. And by common consent the conversation moved on, allowing the delicate frisson of febrile curiosity to migrate in a new direction as they began to discuss the subject of the cabinet minister and his family who were currently holidaying on the island. A few years earlier, a photograph of the then British prime minister and his wife sipping glasses of wine 'on the party island of Ibiza' had been greeted with righteous indignation in the tabloids. So elaborate precautions had been taken to prevent the same censure of the minister stealing front-page news again. And because he was now holed up in one of Giancarlo's *casitas*, everyone present felt themselves somehow deliciously implicated in state secrets.

As Giancarlo shared amusing stories of the elaborate security checks that preceded the minister's arrival, the laughter became charged with something archly conspiratorial. Someone said they would be disappointed not to find the minister included in Saturday's birthday celebrations. 'I can't deny his office have been badgering for an invite,' William said with a wink, 'but it's a hot ticket and, as I keep telling his PA, a line does have to be drawn somewhere.' As laughter rippled through the guests, he helped himself to another glassful of wine and the conversation splintered into smaller groups of twos and threes, some finding enough fellow countrymen within earshot to slip into their native tongues as if into old slippers. Others began rolling joints, or puffing on cigarettes, tipping their heads back to blow languid plumes of smoke at the starry sky. William leant towards Alice with a confiding smile.

'And that, I'm sorry to say, is about the extent of our political discourse here in paradise.'

'Of course,' Charlie smiled at William. 'The miraculous appearance of Alice shouldn't be allowed to eclipse the fact that today is your actual birthday!' At which, cued by a discreet signal from Cressida, Mary appeared at the end of the table holding a cake ablaze with candles. William leant forward to blow them out, beaming at the hearty rendition of 'Happy Birthday', joining in with the laughter and clapping that ensued.

Just as the guests were eagerly reaching out to receive their helping of cake, Alice heard a small, almost subliminal click and the terrace was plunged into darkness. At once there was much thrilled laughter and a small commotion and clatter as several people rose to their feet, bumping into furniture or one another.

'Don't worry. Stay right where you are!' Cressida's voice was only just audible above the hubbub. 'We get these power cuts from time to time. Please bear with us while we dig out some candles.'

William's disembodied voice cut across her, roaring for Rene. And then the lights burst on again, accompanied by a relieved *Ah* from the guests, and there was Rene with a screwdriver in one hand and a torch in the other. Alice accepted the joint someone proffered and took a deep and grateful inhalation. This had to be, without question, the most surreal day of her life. She had no idea what she had been expecting. But not this for sure. She watched William reach out for the bottle of wine again, throwing a furtive glance at Cressida before upending the remainder of the contents into his glass. Then he took up his spoon and tapped the glass. 'Dear friends. Everyone. A final toast if you will – to my long-lost daughter – Alice!'

'To Alice,' the assembled table chorused with feeling, their eyes aglitter with the potent communal swelling of sentiment a well-timed toast can provoke.

The moment Cressida and William retired to their bedroom after dinner, she closed the door behind her, leaning back against it as if to hold the household beyond at bay. Mary had done her evening rounds and the lights were dimmed and the bed turned down, so that the room gave up a glow of comfort. Yet a storm was moving through her as she watched William shed his clothes, a little unsteady on his feet as he stepped out of his trousers, before tripping on his pants, and the evidence of his inebriation only further incensed her. Though she waited for him to turn and ask what was troubling her, he didn't even appear to notice she had entered the room, let alone that she now stood with hands on hips observing him. Instead, now naked apart from his watch, he was padding towards the bed with his head drawing him forward towards the pillow. For one disorientating moment, the room appeared to rush towards her and she spoke with a calm deliberation, as though a measured tone might some-how offset the unravelling of everything.

'So, you *have* been lying to me all along, then . . .'

'What *are you* on about now, Cressida?'

He glugged down water from the glass on the bedside table, exhaling with gusto.

'Alice announced she had been conceived on the island. Just now. In front of everyone.'

'Did she?' He unclipped his watch and set it aside.

'You may have feigned sudden deafness but you know

perfectly well she did. And if Alice was conceived in Ibiza, it could only have happened *after* we met. Not before.'

He picked up a medicine bottle on his side table and shook out some tablets, before gulping them down with another swig of water.

'Honestly. You are quite extraordinary. I don't know how you retain such a forensic memory for dates and events.' He was clambering into bed, pulling the sheet up beneath his chin and settling himself with a cosy little shudder against the pillows.

'Oh please. Don't give me that crap, William. What kind of idiot do you take me for?'

'Look. Darling. There's no point in getting yourself so worked up.' He spoke in the maddeningly condescending tone she had heard him employ on the children when they were being wayward. 'Were you and I seeing each other? Honestly – I can't for the life of me remember now. But I very much doubt it. It all happened a lifetime ago. My God. Most days I can barely even remember what I had for breakfast!'

Enraged, she darted forward and for a moment found herself towering above him, the fact that he was lying prostrate with only his head visible rendering him disconcertingly childlike and vulnerable.

'So I guess you've also conveniently forgotten that the first row we ever had was about your point-blank refusal to let me join you on that trip? How adamant you were it was just a reunion for old college friends. That I'd only feel "out of place". "Trust me," you said. And now I discover that having wanged on so sanctimoniously about trust, you not only went off and fucked someone else, but managed to conceive a child!'

The phrase 'conceived a child' added such a potent note of biblical pathos to her sense of grievance that she found she was trembling from head to toe. 'You cheated on me, William,' she said in a wondering tone, as if to herself. Then turning to him, the words burst from her again as their significance struck home. 'You CHEATED on me . . .' Yet to her utter incredulity, William's eyelids kept closing, and then to add insult to injury, a peculiar subterranean spasm stiffened his jaw and she realised he was struggling to stifle a yawn. For a fleeting moment she was so outraged, she had to wrestle with an overwhelming impulse to pick up the bedside lamp and crash it over his dopey head.

'Let's pursue this in the morning, shall we?' He forced one eye open again. 'It's been one hell of a day . . .' This time, despite his efforts, the yawn escaped him and he had to cover the gaping orifice of his mouth with a paw-like hand.

All at once the velocity of her rage hissed out of her like air from a punctured inflatable. She didn't know what to believe anymore, she said, unexpectedly tearful. If he had lied to her about that, what else had he lied about? The tears that had been welling all day now fell, her anger morphing into self-pity. But already his breath was slowing, as sleep, despite his best efforts to combat it, stole remorselessly upon him. His propensity to sleep in challenging circumstances never failed to astonish her. She sat down on the opposite side of the bed, gathering the sheet in a pleat between her thumb and forefinger, her voice when it came no more than a childlike whisper. 'Why do I have this horrible feeling that you've probably known about her all along?'

The silence expanded around them. His closed eyes fluttered and opened. Finding himself back in the room, he frowned. 'Who?'

'Oh, for fuck's sake, who do you think, William? Alice, of course. *Alice . . .*'

But his eyes only closed again and when he spoke, it was in the somnolent tone of someone conducting a séance. 'You're being utterly ridiculous, Cressida.'

'Please, William. Just tell the truth. That's all I ask . . .'

An even more extended silence, punctured by the long-drawn-out sigh of his breath like the tide going out. Then. 'Alice's email was the first inkling I had. I swear it.' Still his eyes remained closed. How could he be falling asleep when it felt as if the whole world was collapsing?

When Alice's email came, distracted by her own shock, it simply hadn't occurred to her to question either William's protestations of amazement or his explanation of a one-night stand in the lonely months of bachelorhood before they met. It was only now, as she re-ran the moment in her mind's eye, like a police officer reconstructing the scene of a crime, that she wondered if his demeanour hadn't been rather more that of someone who had long anticipated such a message. And now her suspicion coagulated into a conviction of such certainty that she would have howled at the top of her lungs if a vision of Marcus and Kate's startled faces in the next-door bedroom hadn't doused the rising impulse. She stood up and began to pace, turning as soon as she reached the chest of drawers to come back to the bed, all her derision, all her anger bouncing like rubber bullets off this dozing dummy – as if the real William had taken refuge in a lifeless facsimile.

'So. Let's just get this straight, shall we? Despite the fact we had started seeing each other, you insist on going off on this little jolly to Ibiza without me. Where you fuck this woman . . .'

Another sigh, another pause and then again, he spoke in the languorous tone of a sleepwalker from behind the closed eyes.

'You keep saying "this woman". Her name was Jess . . . Alice's mother was called Jess.'

'And you're honestly expecting me to believe that *Jess*' – her mouth dipped in disdain, as if the intimacy of her name had suffused it with a bitter taste – 'never once tried to contact you to tell you she was pregnant with your child?'

'Look. Alice has got her facts muddled, that's all. It was far more likely to have been somewhere like Clerkenwell than Ibiza. I barely spoke to her when we were out here. One moment of madness before you and I met, then off we both went, back to our respective lives. I've told you a million times. Jess was married. She obviously decided it would be easier for her and her husband to keep it to themselves. End of story.'

After that he had turned onto his side and though she continued to try and remonstrate with him, his responses faded away into incomprehensible mutterings, and then a silence broken only by gentle snoring. Sitting hunched on the edge of the bed, Cressida felt more alone than she had ever done in her life before. She thought again of Marcus and Kate lying side by side next door. True teammates, allies. No serpent in their Eden. Usually, the guest room was her bolthole in times of heightened marital conflict. But tonight, there could be no such escape. As William fell deeper into sleep, and his snores escalated into a full-throated nasal rasp, there had been nothing for her to do but take a sleeping tablet and switch off the lights, after which she lay beside him, rigid with rage, until the pill eventually took effect.

2

That evening, the hot winds of the Sahara blew across the sea from Morocco as the desert exhaled upon them while they slept. Later, the winds escalated into a small storm, tearing at the branches of the trees and rattling the doors in their frames. But by the time dawn broke, a complete calm was restored. A stillness so complete, it made the gardens appear like a painted backdrop.

Through her window as Cressida dressed, she had watched Mary stooping to retrieve the scattered outdoor cushions and right fallen garden chairs, while Rene swept away the light dusting of desert sand that now powdered every surface. What a ceaseless commitment the whole thing required, Cressida thought, her energy momentarily sagging as she swept her hair into a ponytail. A bit like producing a daily stage show. By the time the household emerged from their bedrooms, everything would be as spick and span as it had been when everyone retired.

Roused from their beds by Mary's timid tap at their door, very soon the guests had all congregated about the ample breakfast she had laid out on the terrace. A jovial banter was sparking amongst them as they savoured their first meal of the day and eyed the luminous early morning sky, beginning to take in the prospect of an adventure on William's boat. At length, once they had all been fed and watered, they were chivvied into the jeep, whose boot was already stacked by Rene with bags of towels, sun cream and snorkelling equipment.

Cressida came to peer in at them through the open window of the car.

'Does someone have a credit card to pay for lunch?' she asked, knowing perfectly well what the answer would be. Experience had taught her that their perfectly competent guests tended to abdicate any semblance of personal autonomy for the duration of their stay.

'Shit.' Marcus bolted from the car. 'Let me just grab my wallet, will you.'

'Seasickness pills?'

'Oh, oh, for goodness' sake, yes thank you – sorry everyone!' Now it was Kate's turn to clamber out, flapping her hands in alarm, her short stature meaning she had to drop with difficulty from the back seat to the ground. 'So sorry guys. One sec.'

Two more guests hurried back into the house behind her – a pale teenager emerging from his torpor to an abrupt realisation of the impossibility of a day without his headphones. Followed by someone who all at once feared that they must either retrieve their magic jellyfish sting remedy or risk life and limb. For a few perilous moments, the spirit of adventure was superseded by a generalised panic at the prospect of imminent jeopardy on the high seas – and then at last, all the fluster had subsided, and as the doors were slammed shut, Cressida could resume her gracious hostess smile and wave her hand in relieved farewell as the jeep shot off down the driveway in a spatter of gravel, and a chirpy toot from Charlie at the wheel.

The sound of the departing horn jolted Alice from complex dreams and for a moment she had no idea where she was. She looked about her in confusion at the Babar the Elephant prints on the wall. She took in the wooden beamed ceiling, where the ebony fan whirred.

You are in the house of William Gifford. Your father.

'But I have a father already.'

You know what I mean. Your biological father. The man whose genes you share.

'I don't care about that. It was Pete who raised me.'

Then why have you come?

She got out of bed and switched off the fan. Bars of brilliant white light spilling from the edges of the shutters and across the plastered walls.

'I'm not sure . . .'

She went to the double doors and pushed them open, looking out over the gardens that stretched in manicured lines to the distant boundary walls, becoming conscious of the temperate morning air passing over her bare skin.

'But I think it was almost certainly a mistake.'

She recalled Cressida pressing her to join everyone on a boat trip somewhere. She had resisted, the prospect filling her with dread.

'I only know that I have nothing in common with this man. Nothing in common with these people.'

She looked at the deep ultramarine mountains on the far horizon. The flush of rose rising low in the sky just behind them. From the trees of the forest beyond the boundary walls came the call and whir of birds, their darting, flitting forms in continual airborne motion. Then the velvet crooning of a turtle dove so mellifluous that she pulled on a bikini and stepped out, drawn by their melody, into the garden.

William glimpsed Alice several times from afar as he walked about dealing with the first work calls of the day. She was wandering up and down the avenues of fruit trees, often bending to examine a plant – and once he saw her standing at the boundary wall, absorbed by the distant views of the sea. As soon as his call ended, he went in search of her, noting the rumble of the first delivery truck of the day coming down the drive and, not long after, the noise of carpentry work resuming. He was just rounding a corner when he almost collided with her.

'Alice! A very good morning to you! You resisted the boat trip, then!'

As he put his phone away in his pocket, they fell quite easily into step.

'Why go anywhere else,' she said. 'I mean it's paradise here.'

'Believe it or not, the whole garden only went in a year ago! Literally everything you see – all these magnificent old olives, all these mature cypress trees, the whole lawn all rolled up like a carpet – everything arrived on the back of lorries. Et voila! Instant garden. The secret lies in these ingenious watering systems you can install now.'

As if on cue, there was a rapid agitation of liquid being propelled at great speed down scores of subterranean tubes before being released in pattering cascades amongst the shrubbery. Then, as William and Alice retreated in haste to the safety of the gravel path, row after row of twirling sprinkler heads rose up from the emerald lawn, emitting a fine spray of water, and as one row finished and vanished beneath the grass again, another row rose up in its stead, appearing and disappearing with an eerie military precision across the vast expanse of turf. They watched from the safety of the path until the circuit was completed and the loud hissing of water rushing through compressed tubes ceased as abruptly as it had begun.

'Oof.' She was grimacing. 'You must be getting through a hell of a lot of water. No wonder everything's so green.'

'Don't get me started on the water situation,' William said, shaking droplets from his sandals. 'We've had a complete nightmare trying to access a reliable supply. Originally, we drew all our water from the old well. But we'd no sooner put this garden in than we realised that the damn thing was running dry. So we had to drill for a new one. It took a few false starts, but eventually we thought we'd cracked it. Look, I'll show you. The second well is just through here.'

Beyond the drystone walls they skirted, the forest rose in a primal and impenetrable thicket. They passed through a grove of orange trees where the noise from the cicadas was so loud he felt as much as heard their vibration.

'No sooner was this one up and running than it dried up too. Un-friggin'-believable.'

William opened up the wooden doors and handed Alice a pebble. She leant forward to release it into the well's dark depths, waiting until the silence was broken by the subdued and distant echo of stone striking stone, a sound so resonantly hollow, it appeared to emanate from the very bowels of the earth. She stared for some while into the shadows before letting out a deep sigh.

'I see . . .' she said at last, inscrutable thoughts turning behind her eyes. Observing her troubled expression, the faintest unease stirred in him. *What exactly was it she saw?*

'Problems in paradise, right?' he said in an upbeat tone.

'I always tell Cress when she complains about the endless setbacks – no one ever said that living the dream would be easy.'

Alice glanced back the way they had just come at the glossy wet lawn and he followed her gaze, the beads of water that winked and glittered everywhere appearing suddenly like fistfuls of carelessly discarded jewels. She turned back to scan his face, apparently perplexed by his levity.

'It's not really such a big deal,' he said, sounding more defensive than he had intended. 'Just means we now have to pay a fortune to get daily trucks of water delivered from one of the desalinisation plants. But – hey – what can you do, right?'

What can you do? A rhetorical question he used so often in daily conversation he would never in the usual scheme of things have noted it. Yet today, with Alice's eyes fixed upon him, the unease lingered. Yet another winter had gone by without rain and although it was still only June, already the island was as dry as a bone, the paths in places no more than drifting dust bowls, while the verdant winter grasses of the *campo* had long since withered away.

'Desalinisation plants are a disaster for marine life, you know,' Alice said in a cool tone. 'Anyone who thinks they offer some kind of magical solution is living in cloud cuckoo land.'

In the hope of currying favour, William abruptly changed tack. Perhaps she would like to take a look at their permaculture patch, he said. See for herself how they were trying to do their bit for the environment. They had even been thinking about investing in some beehives, he went on, omitting to add that, for reasons now lost to him, he had only mocked the idea.

They came to a nursery garden where an abundant trelliswork of vegetables stretched away in riotous rows. At the far end of one of the lines, Mary was filling a trug, and she bobbed her head in apology when she saw them, hunching over her basket as if to minimise her presence.

The truth was he'd never quite grasped what a perma-culture patch actually entailed. It was Cressida's thing, really. But so many of the people they knew were now installing one, it had seemed necessary to show how they were moving with the times and had instructed their staff to take appropriate action.

Alice looked about, surveying it all with evident pleasure, and he received her approval with relief. She bent to examine the aubergines now swelling and shading into purple as they lay in their straw beds, running a tender finger along the sheeny flesh.

He felt things had eased a little between them as they resumed their stroll. 'We only moved to Ibiza after much agonising. We'd spent so many holidays sitting in some charming little bar, sipping wine in a beach restaurant, wishing we didn't have to leave. So one day in a moment of madness, I put our house on the market and booked the kids into the international school. And next thing I know – here we all are!'

Every now and then he bent to wrench out a coarse snaking type of grass that had woven its way through the finer green blades, tutting under his breath as he did so. He couldn't seem to help himself, rushing forward whenever evidence of the offending interloper snagged his eye, so that the fistful soon grew into an unwieldy wet clump in his hand.

'Life here is a delightful bubble. The troubles of the world can seem very far away. You hear the news and think holy shit, is that really what's going on out there? It can be tempting just to switch the news off again. Pull up the drawbridge. Pour yourself another glass of rosé.' He paused, trying to read her. That hint of a frown hovering again. How to explain that flip comments had always been his stock-in-trade? 'Guess that might sound a bit cavalier to an activist like you . . .'

They passed the swimming pool, where Rene was lying on his belly trying to fish something out with a net. Further on they passed a chill-out area heaped with cushions that usually housed reclining guests, beyond it sun-dappled orchards stretching away. William bent to wrench out another clump of the rogue grass as they reached the far perimeters of the garden. Before he could forestall her, Alice had stepped towards a little wooden gate and swung it open. They found themselves at the foot of a hidden pool that gleamed like a liquefied inversion of the sky.

'You have two pools!' she exclaimed.

'Well. This one's a lap pool . . . Cressida decided it would help get me in shape. Which of course it would if I ever actually had time to use the bloody thing!' He patted his pot belly with a rueful gesture. 'All totally illegal, I'm afraid.'

Again the cool eyes upon him. 'But you built it anyway.'

He forced a laugh. 'Look. I'd hate you to get the wrong impression. You shouldn't take too much notice of what my friends were saying about me last night. I'm really not the cavalier wheeler-dealer type they like to make me out as, you know! They were just trying to wind you up. That's all.'

Alice nodded, apparently deep in thought, before walking to the far end of the pool and pulling off her T-shirt. She dived headlong, skimming the bottom until she reached the end, where William stood watching. She emerged just a few feet from him, to float on her back and expel a spout of water.

'I have a bunch of questions for you,' she said, one eye closed against the blinding sky above him.

'Ah, I had a funny feeling you hadn't come just to wish me happy birthday!' He managed with some difficulty to hold his smile. 'Please. Ask away. It's important we feel able to be entirely open with one another.' He was just stooping to pull forward one of the sunloungers when his phone began to vibrate in his hand and he glanced at it with a leap of relief he hoped was not too obvious. He pulled a face when he saw his chief investor's name flash across the screen, faking annoyance. 'Excuse me. I'm afraid I'll have to take this.'

She pulled herself up and out of the pool in a single twisting motion, opening her mouth to make some rejoinder, but his phone was already clamped to his ear.

'Hey buddy. What's up?' He walked away, leaning in to the phone with a charming smile, his outstretched hand gesturing his delight, as if addressing a caller only he could see.

Cressida cast about for a suitable epithet to calm herself, but fragments of last night's terrible row with William kept returning to torment her. Endlessly revised versions of the things she should and could have said chased about her brain; the searing riposte that would have more definitively established his culpability. The smart put-down so unerring it would cut him to the quick every time he recalled it. Once she had finished writing out the two hundred placement cards in a careful hand, she turned to her list. But even as she crossed off tasks from the top, she only found herself adding new ones to the bottom.

She took a moment to exhale. *I choose to be calm and centred, regardless of the situation.* She had always threaded her life with a myriad affirmative gestures and self-help phrases designed to ward off the darker uncertainties; like the jokey emojis that adorned all her texts. *Everything happens for a reason* was a phrase she was fond of employing, despite the fact it always irked William. I've no idea what that *actually* means, Cressida, he had more than once protested when he happened to overhear her employing the phrase. *Good things happen to those who wait, Life doesn't give you anything you can't handle* were other reliable standbys that could offer fleeting comfort. When they first moved to Ibiza, she had transcribed the line *Every new day is a chance to change your life* on a Post-it note and stuck it to the bathroom mirror, where it remained as a morning pick-me-up, until it fluttered loose one day and was thrown away by Mary.

Determined to make a success of the move, Cressida had hired someone to teach her Kundalini yoga and booked a series of workshops on Happiness and Harmony. Like everything she undertook, she gave herself wholeheartedly to this new chapter, and for a while – and despite William's undisguised scepticism – she had dabbled with the teachings of an Indian guru named Saraswati – though he had been the first of her new age experimentations to fall quietly by the wayside.

Since their relocation here, she had listened with an alert unease at a number of dinner parties while exponents of the island's frequent all-night *ayahuasca* ceremonies extolled the benefits the South American hallucinogenic had afforded them, benefits that apparently ranged from insight into the true nature of the universe to the shedding of past traumas. Its many proponents argued that far from being a recreational drug, *ayahuasca* was a plant-based medicine whose purgative qualities facilitated a healing of the spirit. An Austrian self-styled high priestess, together with a shaman regularly flown over from Peru, presided over many of the ceremonies that in recent years had become such a key feature of the island's under-the-radar events. Both William and Cressida were united in viewing the prospect of undergoing such an ordeal with an alarm that only deepened as it became apparent that *ayahuasca* had created a subtle schism in the island's expat community, with the proponents who embraced it on one side and the dissenters like themselves who resisted on the other. In evading the ceremonies, they sensed that they were viewed as closed-minded and in time found themselves subtly sidelined by certain social circles. It seemed that in this bastion of liberalism, spurning opportunities to expand your consciousness was one of the few ways left to socially transgress.

She was fascinated by the history of the island. Besieged for hundreds of years by pirates, together with wave after wave of invaders, the Ibicenco population had been forced to remain small and porous. So when the artists and political refuseniks came to escape Franco, followed a little later by young Americans wanting to dodge the Vietnam War, all were readily assimilated. As were the hippies who stopped off en route from Goa and Morocco in the 1960s and 70s and, liking what they found, soon settled and put down roots. It was said that when the hippies first arrived in the 1960s, the Ibicencos had dubbed them *els peluts* – the hairy ones – little realising the hairy ones would stay on to become such a ubiquitous part of the island scene.

As a result of their legacy, she could choose between a head-spinning diversity of esoteric alternative therapies:

tantric sex workshops jostling for space with rebirthing classes, an exuberant and often arcane cross-fusion of spiritual disciplines that offered a cultural mash-up of anything from Native American spirit guides to Eastern practices and pagan mysticism. Cressida had even been to visit the remote cave not far from their home where the goddess Tanit, brought to the island two thousand years earlier by the Carthaginians, was still actively worshipped. She had written a little note to Tanit asking her for inspiration on her way forward and left it buried amongst the heaped offerings on the altar.

The modern world might be in uproar. Christianity might be a spent force. But even amongst this wealth of alternative practices, she could find no road map to navigate by.

She pushed the name cards away and covered her face with her hands. Then, coming to an abrupt decision, she tiptoed down the corridor to Alice's room. She gave a tentative tap on the door but as she expected, there was no response. Mary had told her she had seen William showing Alice around the garden. The door was half ajar and she pushed it wider before stepping into the empty room with a thumping heart. She stood looking about and after a moment opened the cupboard Mary had cleared for Alice, where she contemplated the lone T-shirt lying folded on the shelf. Then she closed the cupboard again and made herself turn back for the door, stroking and patting her arms, walking herself away.

Don't be silly Cressida. Come on now. You can't just go rifling through people's private things like this.

But halfway to the door she wheeled all the way round again, as if her cantering heart were now propelling her like a clockwork toy, and, snatching up Alice's backpack, fished through its contents until she found what she had come for. Alice's passport. Her hands were trembling as she flicked to the information page. A judder went through her very being when she found it. Just as she had thought. Exactly as she suspected. Alice was born in February. Precisely nine months after that Ibiza reunion. Renewed fury rose to choke her all over again.

'Oh!'

She spun about to find Alice standing frozen in the doorway, her eyes rounded in surprise. Cressida felt the bag and passport slip through her bloodless fingers and fall to the floor.

'What gives you the right . . .' Cressida heard her voice so high and shrill. 'How dare you . . .' Alice's astonished face goaded her on.

'Did you never stop to think what impact your turning up here unannounced would have on me? Or my children? Or does your noble mission to save the world give you carte blanche to do exactly as you fucking well please?'

Alice stared at Cressida for some moments before advancing towards her, the abrupt suspension of polite social discourse making anything seem possible. Cressida shrank back with a squawk of alarm, half raising an arm to defend herself. But Alice only snatched up her backpack and passport from the floor, hugging them to her chest as she backed away towards the door.

'Thanks for the warm welcome.' Then she turned on her heel and was gone.

Cressida's heart was still hammering as she went upstairs to her bathroom and patted concealer along the dark crescent of each eye – *a mini miracle: brightens your eyes and your spirits* – and stepped away from the mirror. They would just have to get through the next two days. Batten down the hatches and put their best face to the world. She tried to apply lipstick but her hand trembled so much it took several attempts. Then she lifted the corners of her mouth into her brightest hostess smile.

'Every day I have the power to choose,' she said to the mirror through clenched teeth. 'And today, I choose happiness.'

Mary had gone over the numbers several more times after the guests had departed for their boat trip. She had covered two pages with outgoings and incomings and projected earnings, all inscribed in the manner taught to her by the diligent supply teacher in the village school. But none of the figures could be made to tally with the sum they needed. So much for the lady she had hired to say prayers for them every Sunday.

'*Bahala na,*' Rene had said, observing Mary's despair, and planting a kiss on her head as he passed by. *It's all up to God.*

She put the papers away, before bowing to the statue of Mama Mary and setting off on her bedroom rounds.

Though to Cressida and William she might appear as meek as a mouse, to her husband and family in the Philippines, Mary was considered an indomitable matriarch. In fact Cressida and William knew so little about their maid they had no idea that even the name they called her was not in fact her real one. She had been baptised and raised as Mahalic, but decided to anglicise it for expediency's sake once she arrived in Ibiza. Neither did they know that she'd had to leave school at eleven to start work in Manila as a babysitter when her father found himself unable to afford the fees to send her on to secondary education. Though she was smaller than her peers, the spark of life burnt so brightly in her that she found to her great surprise once she reached puberty, she had attracted many suitors. Amongst them Rene, who courted her with quiet determination. When he took her to the cinema, her father insisted her nephew accompany them. But in time, impressed both by his persistence and the prospects his engineering degree promised, she had turned down her other suitors and agreed to marry him. Once they had tied the knot and she had given birth to their child, Angel, she was determined her daughter should have the means to study to be a nurse and make a life beyond the grinding rural poverty she herself had known. So, despite her mother's steadfast opposition, Mary had left Angel in her care when she was just a year old before setting off to seek her fortune abroad.

In the main guest suite, a silk kaftan had been laid out on the bed in readiness for the evening's festivities. With its arms outstretched, its hem skirted a pair of brand-new high heels set side by side on the floor. It was as if the wearer had lain down only to vanish into thin air, she thought, leaving just their outer garments to mark their passing. As Mary stood in the doorway, trying to decide where to start, she saw that Marcus and Kate had unpacked and laid everything out so painstakingly that for once there was no need for her to pick up or fold anything. She walked through the room with her feather duster at the ready, taking care not to move anything, stepping so lightly she felt no more than a mote of dust.

She had always relished her liberty to inhabit the private spaces of the house without any requirement to actually interact with their occupants. She would probably never exchange a word with Marcus and Kate Morrison, but she would nonetheless have shaken out the rumpled sheets on which they slept and passed a duster over their most intimate possessions. In doing so, she might come across the evidence of their lovemaking or a smudge of menstrual blood. She might scoop up nail clippings left inexplicably in a neat pile on the bedside table, or gather up discarded undergarments from the floor. Once she had retrieved a mysterious cylinder-shaped object from under a pillow that began to vibrate as she examined it. Having managed with some difficulty to quiet it again, she turned it over and over for clues, before returning it with a peculiar feeling of having been privy to something illicit. Even the exposed contents of the open suitcase on the footstool offered an implicit assertion of faith in her discretion. As did the thick pile of folded banknotes beside the heavy gold wristwatch coiled on the chest of drawers, and the brand-new laptop charging on the floor. These trappings of casual affluence inspired her to carry herself with a certain gravity as she moved about them. Just as the priest heard her confession without judgement, so she in turn was privy to the secret lives of strangers.

In the bathroom, Marcus and Kate had overlooked only the toilet bowl in their careful attention to order. She swept a lone pubic hair from the toilet seat before sawing at the flecks of faeces that had stuck fast to the vitreous enamel of the interior with the lavatory brush. Otherwise the expensive bottles of toiletries and cosmetics had been set out on the stone counter with a fetishistic precision. Beside them stood a handsome leather jewellery box, inside which she discovered a pirate's bounty of rubies and sapphires, topaz and diamonds set in gold. She picked up one of the rings to better admire it, and then another and another, before, unable to resist, sliding them onto each of her fingers in turn, her breath coming in quick apprehensive inhalations at what she knew perfectly well was a transgression. But she had watched Marcus and Kate set off for the boat trip and it was only the certainty that there would be no interruption that emboldened her. Even so, the bedroom door was ajar and she kept her ears tuned for any footsteps in the corridor. She turned to her reflection in the mirror to fluff up her hair in that fey manner Cressida often employed.

Could you, Mary, would you mind frightfully, Mary, I know it's such a bore . . .

She noted the dark rings of sleeplessness about her eyes. Angel's confirmation ceremony was only three months away now. In their last Skype conversation her daughter had pressed her to say whether they were coming and Mary had been evasive, loath to either dash her hopes or build them. For some while she had been working at one of the new organic farms on her day off and doing some bookkeeping for a friend in the evenings in order to try and raise the funds. It was dispiriting not to have more to show for it.

As a child, she and her siblings had slept on the floor beneath a mosquito net. Every morning on waking their first chore was to collect water from the community well. She had felt yoked to the land and yearned to be free. But even in exile, solvency still eluded her. A series of catastrophic typhoons had wiped out their rice crop in the Philippines. The cost of fertiliser was soaring. And there were so many family members who needed help with medical and educational costs. But one day, one day, the time would come when they could return to the Philippines and take up full-time management of their land and livestock. When they would be reunited with Angel. They often referred to this long-awaited homecoming and the prospect of it never failed to bolster their resolve.

It was now two years since she and Rene had last managed
to get home to see their daughter, arriving laden with presents
to much rejoicing. The lurch of delight when she was reunited
with Angel was always underscored by wistfulness at how
their daughter had grown during their long separations.
Despite their regular Skype conversations, the flesh and blood
reality was always disconcerting.

But at least her mother and daughter were now installed in
the modest brick farmhouse with the smart metal roof she and
Rene had paid to have built on the outskirts of their village.
On their last visit, it had been a source of great satisfaction to
sit on the crackling protective plastic covers of the three-piece
suite and submerge themselves, if only for a brief while, in the
tangible fruits of their long exile.

When Mary first came to Ibiza, Rene was still studying as
an engineer and her overseas employment had been intended
only as a temporary measure until he had graduated and
found work. But when the funds for his studies dried up, he
had decided to join her in Spain instead. Since then, compared
to their friends and family who had taken up posts in the
Middle East, life had been kind. Though Mary missed her
daughter and often shed quiet tears for her, at least their
hours were honoured and their day off respected. They lived
in modest windowless quarters in the basement of William
and Cressida's main outhouse, filled with furniture rejected
from the main house or built by Rene in his spare time. The
many framed photographs of Angel, together with her school

certificates and crayon drawings, made it a shrine to their absent child. But it was also a space in which the melancholy of living in exile was somewhat tempered by a radio always tuned to FM91.5 Metro Manila, while the satellite television brought them Filipino soap operas, which they watched while cooking dishes from home and conversing companionably in Cebuano.

Before William and Cressida's permanent relocation to Ibiza, while the house was still being finished, there had been long periods when Rene and Mary had had the place to themselves. During those months, the fruit and vegetables from the garden were theirs to consume and the odd judiciously chosen bottle of wine from the cellar an illicit treat for high days and holidays. But the culture of moderation instilled in them from their earliest days by the church meant any liberties they might take were always modest ones. When Christmas came, in a moment of uncharacteristic daring, they had even temporarily moved out of their basement and into the main house, where they took the handsome guest suite next door to the master suite in a gesture that was as much expedient as it was deferential, since any residual traces of their residency were far less likely to betray them.

Without the eyes of their employers upon them, they had moved about their upgraded sleeping quarters and kitchen with a looser step, sometimes bickering and sometimes bantering in Cebuano, and allowing the plates to clatter as they set them down. But it had nearly all unravelled when a friend of Cressida's stopped by unannounced and almost stumbled upon them sitting at the table on the terrace in the winter sunshine, just as Cressida and William might have done, idly gossiping while enjoying the remnants of *Pancit Luglug*. Both had leapt from their seats at the sound of someone calling, and by the time the neighbour – a cheerful Danish woman – had rounded the corner holding aloft the book she was returning, she found Rene at the top of a hastily positioned ladder innocently handing down dead branches to Mary, who was gathering them in her apron with an industrious air. If the Danish woman hadn't been in such a rush, she might perhaps have noted the dirty dishes on the table or paused to wonder why Rene was sawing at such robust branches with a flimsy cutlery knife. But fortunately for them, despite her merry smile and cheerful greeting, their presence was such a ubiquitous aspect of so many of the affluent households on the island that, like most expats, she barely noted them.

Thinking she heard a movement in the corridor, Mary hastily slid the rings from her fingers, the many gleaming facets of the diamonds, rubies and emeralds clicking against one another as they tumbled. Only one ring remained in her palm, an uncut diamond, much less showy and distinctive than the rest. *Would it really be missed amongst so many?* She examined the hallmark. Imagine you exchanged it for money. Imagine you used that money to go home for Angel's confirmation.

Would God judge you for it – or would the purpose to which you put it offer some mitigation?

She let it fall back amongst its companions. But it was a false alarm. Someone's bare feet, heading in the opposite direction, moving away down the corridor towards the stairs. From the heartfelt sigh, she knew at once it must be Cressida. She became aware of the time. The children's video would be ending. She must go and get them ready for a trip somewhere. Keeping them out of their mother's way had become her primary current preoccupation. Like a squirrel storing nuts for the winter months, Mary had spent the past few weeks striving diligently to lay down a store of goodwill with her employer and, with a queasy flutter of apprehension, knew she had to capitalise on it soon.

Descending the stairs, she heard William calling out a farewell and caught a glimpse of his car reversing, before it vanished down the drive. As she made her way towards the children's room, different windows afforded a quick inventory of the household. On the west lawn, the Bedouin tent looked resplendent. Through another window, the rows of empty sunloungers faced out over the pool, where a bright pink inflatable flamingo floated serenely up and down. On the north side she watched Alice and one of the workers confer, the man pointing in the direction of the sea, appearing to map out a route with hand gestures, before Alice raised a jaunty wave of thanks and set off towards the gate, swinging her bag onto her back as she went and stepping out with a determined stride.

William took each turn of the mountain road at the very edge of a speed that was wise, his awareness of potential jeopardy from the precipitous drops to his right arousing just enough adrenaline to revive him from his hangover and counter the leapfrogging of his mind.

As he drove he reviewed his conversation with Alice, ruminating on the subterranean moments of unease. On his return, he would find time to sit down with her as he had promised. She had a perfect right to understand more about her past. Of course she did. Even if the questions led him back to a past on which he had long attempted to wrestle the door closed. An image of a dangling nylon thread came to him. In the old days – in the days when he'd still bought his suits from the High Street – one tug on that irritating nylon thread protruding from a hem could cause the whole line to unravel in a series of infinitesimally tiny lurches as each stitch undid itself in turn. It was Alice's casually innocent assertion she had been conceived here in Ibiza that had set the unravelling in motion. Impossible to say where that incendiary little gem of information might lead now. The cat was certainly out of the bag.

For a while he forced himself to focus only on the twisting road that flew towards him, absorbing himself in the challenge of keeping the wheel angled to meet it while his foot held the pedal at the accelerator's optimum biting point. This need to move forward with maximum haste was one he sought in all aspects of his life, regardless of whether or not haste was actually required.

After the long search for the house of their dreams, they had eventually settled in this most northerly and remote part of the island; a steeply mountainous region as far from the notorious excesses of the south as it was possible to be. Indeed, the road he now navigated had been built just eight years before he was born. Before that the whole region had been so cut off from the rest of the island it was known as the 'lost valley' and, for the isolated farming community who lived there, it had been quicker to take a boat down the coast than to navigate the meandering shepherds' trails that ran southwards over the mountains. William had been charmed by this account, as relayed by the estate agent who had taken them to see the derelict old finca that was now their home.

As he rounded the final curve at the top of the mountain, a stationary car blocking his lane flashed into view, forcing William to swerve to the opposite side to avoid a collision. *Jesus!* A man – an Ibicenco – was standing beside the broken-down car, flapping at the dense black smoke rising from the open bonnet. At the sight of potential rescue, the man bent to pick up something from a basket at his feet, and raised his hands in an imploring request for help. He appeared to be brandishing a lobster. Though their eyes briefly locked, William's need to keep his foot on the accelerator was greater than any instinct to stop. He glanced in his rear-view mirror. For a fraction of a second, framed by the mirror, he saw the man's expression of despair as his hands dropped to his sides again, before the twist of the road caused him to vanish from view as quickly as he had appeared. *Mother of God . . .* He slowed his pace a little and turned up the music, feeling his heart rate beginning to subside.

Once he reached the little village of Sant Joan, his spirits leapt as they always did with the kind of relief that only someone with such an essentially urban disposition could feel at finding themselves, out of the wild hinterlands and back amongst the hustle and bustle of people. Though in truth, the charms of such a modest village were too finite to do much more than temporarily assuage the feeling of exile. He had been dismayed to discover that instead of growing easier, the more time passed, the more onerous the remoteness of their house became to him. On a recent trip to London, he had arrived so early for a business lunch at the Wolseley, he decided to kill some time in Fortnum & Mason's, where he browsed for tea and observed the shop assistants in their black coat-tails with a pang of patriotism he knew was absurd even as it felled him.

'Might I possibly be of any assistance, sir?' a smiling member of staff had asked him with the most charming and deferential of head tilts. The elaborate bells of the Fortnum & Mason clock were chiming their dainty tinkle as he left. He had passed Hatchards with its mouthwatering display of books. Then the Royal Academy, whose sun-dappled courtyard gave off an odour of refinement that hinted at the hidden wellsprings of culture within. And in that moment, he couldn't for the life of him recall why he had ever felt compelled to flee it all. The feeling of something valuable that had slipped just out of reach weighed on him for days after his return to Ibiza. *How perverse to have chosen to remove oneself from all the things that once gave life its fizz!*

You could spot the expats a mile away, swanning about in their straw hats and hessian-soled espadrilles, play-acting a bucolic life of yore. Yet it was highly debatable how bucolic the locals' lives had ever in reality been. He soon discovered that the years when starvation forced generations of young people to seek work overseas were still fresh in the Ibicenco psychology. Which was why so many were happy to relinquish generations of family history in exchange for a modern life in one of the islands ever expanding towns. The convenience of mains water and electricity, together with the novelty of shops within walking distance, exerted a strong pull. Meanwhile, couples like Cressida and William, having purchased the Ibicenco's run-down family inheritance, set to work with enthusiasm to negotiate the labyrinthine regulations required to renovate a house without even the most basic of amenities. And these two groups, one fleeing the city, and the other the countryside, were ships that met only in the office of the notary. A cursory shake of the hand, a quick signature on the requisite property deeds, before they headed off in opposite directions. What the native Ibicencos made of this latter-day invasion of gringos, William had no idea, since they remained a tribe apart, by and large only glimpsed from afar, a short sturdily built people at work in their fields or emerging all spick and span in their finest clothes from the church service on Sunday. In his occasional business encounters with them, William had discovered, much to his chagrin, that parting the Ibicenco from their land involved immense persistence. Pedro, the farmer who had eventually consented to sell him the coastal plot at Cala Conta, was the descendant of six generations all called Pedro too, and negotiations had been protracted. Smiling in perpetual wily amusement at William's determination to secure his land, and with an unlit cigar always clamped in the corner of his mouth, Pedro had neither budged an inch on price nor made a single concession on detail.

Arriving at long last at Cala Conta, William got out of the car and stretched his cramped legs as he contemplated the long stretch of rugged coastline. *One of the most desirable and least developed areas of Ibiza*, his advance sales publicity boasted. And for once it was more than mere marketing hyperbole – for this was by any standards an unusually magnificent site with wide views across the sea to the south-west. The plot was naturally flat, just as if Mother Nature had always had a project of this kind in mind. Once built, the rows of villas would hunker down into the land and appear to have been there since time immemorial. *A playground to the world. The discerning buyer will enjoy stunning sunset views, while cocooned in the comfort of their state-of-the-art abodes, finished to the highest technological standards and offering maximum luxury, security and style.* Something out of nothing. Like a conjuring trick.

It was ironic that once he settled here, it had been his avowed intention that the island should remain a refuge from business. But as houses sprouted up everywhere, he caught the heady whiff of a gold rush and believing he could do it better – do it even perhaps with integrity – had begun, despite himself, to dabble. How was a man with a nose for these things to resist when there were so many lucrative deals to be done? A land agent offering a 'once in a lifetime opportunity on a very unique spot'. Insider information on a seedy leisure complex for sale, not only situated in an area now on the up, but also in a municipality (and here his informant would drop their voice confidingly) in which the local mayor would be willing to bend the commercial restrictions for only a modest five per cent of the eventual sales price.

As his understanding of the myriad ways to stretch the regulations and grease the right palms grew, so increasingly irresistible windows of opportunity revealed themselves to him. He soon learnt that the continual shifting of the government between right and left meant he could buy land cheaply while the left was in power, imposing their usual stringent moratorium on any further development, in the confident knowledge that four years later he could embark on a building jamboree once the right returned and promptly suspended all restrictions again. And before he knew it, despite his best intentions, a bit of land banking here and a little property speculation there had accumulated into a substantial portfolio.

He kicked at a cluster of fleshy-leaved succulents that had somehow drawn sufficient sustenance from the rocky ground, then glanced at his watch. He had been in such a rush to get out of the house, he had arrived well in advance of his team and now found himself in the rare position of having time on his hands. Time to reflect was an unaccustomed feeling – and not an entirely welcome one. He observed his surveyors in their fluorescent jackets as they worked their way along the projected elevations with their altimeters and tried to turn his thoughts from the hornets' nest that awaited him at home. He eyed the scattered bathers who had spread their towels on the reddish sands, from where they could contemplate the unique aquamarine of the sea. A small crowd of young Spanish hippies, with skin as tanned as polished cherrywood, had just arrived. They were observing the surveyors work as they undressed, conversing in satirical undertones. One of them rubbed his thumb and forefinger together as if savouring banknotes, with a disdain that made all his companions hoot with laughter. Then with a shake of their heads, they bolted for the sea, leaping headlong one after the other, as if to cleanse themselves of something contaminating.

The cicadas were rattling like gunfire in the hedgerows as Alice strode under the full blaze of the midday sun, the dazzling intensity of light tinging her peripheral vision with a subtle hallucinatory jitter.

'What the hell is her problem?' she enquired of the great indifferent wilderness. 'What kind of person does that?' she said, taking swipes at the tall stems of giant fennel that sprouted on either side of the trail. But after a while, as the liberation of walking stole upon her, her anger began to recede as she attended to the ceaseless whirring of creatures from the hedgerows and took in the vigour of the vegetation that sprouted in such abundance on either side. A tangle of delicate Mediterranean aromatics entwined with thorny African cactus. Here she was on this tiny dot of land, somewhere between Europe and Africa. In another life she might take a ferry on to Morocco. Hitch-hike her way into a whole new adventure. Flee all the trouble that awaited her in the UK. To quell the familiar leap of dread, she began to sing, beating time with her hands and feet.

The idea of following the track from the house down through the forest to the sea had seemed such a simple one. But the trail kept splitting, so that each time she had to select one turning over the other, it soon became apparent how impossible it would be to ever retrace her footsteps. After a while she forgot everything but moving through the land, the swing of pelvis throwing forth first one foot and then the other, lulling her into a trance-like state in which she soon became no more than a receiver of sight and sound.

She had been walking for some while when the track began to climb uphill again, and the woods enclosed her, the astringent scent of pine resin rousing her a little. It was several degrees cooler in the shade. The branches of each tree were furred with curlicues of lichen and arched overhead like the complex rafters of a church. It occurred to her with a start that she ought to text William to let him know she had gone. But her phone showed no signal when she took it out. Already the memory of his manicured kingdom struck her as improbable. Those myopic guests. The upstairs and downstairs of it all. The unselfconscious affluenza. She returned the phone to her backpack and stepped out into the heat of the day again.

In her gap year she had lived in Wales in a bender she'd built herself on land a farmer had lent her beside the banks of a stream. She had cooked over an open fire and washed in the stream. Each day was shaped by the basic tasks of survival. She would forage for wild food, supplemented with any unwanted produce from the farmer, and at night taught herself how to play a ukulele that her father had bought her. To live alone, and in such close proximity with the natural world, had awoken a deep wellspring of affinity that had remained within her ever since. And somewhere along the way she mislaid the trick of familiarity that had always allowed her to accept the constructed world and instead began to experience a rising panic at the encroachment of urban creep upon the land. And to grieve for all that had been lost and how little was being done to preserve what was left.

'One of the penalties of an ecological education is that one lives alone in a world of wounds,' Aldo Leopold had written. It described something so hitherto unarticulated in her, her whole being had blanched when she came across his words in the library one day. She was meant to be reading about Chaucer but she could no longer recall to what end. Increasingly, the ecological texts that now preoccupied her study hours overwhelmed her. For a while the feeling of living in a world of wounds engulfed her. She briefly consulted a therapist, who used a term she had never heard before to describe her state of mind. 'Eco grief.' But how could anyone live with the crushing reality of species extinction, rising sea levels, ever escalating temperatures, the mass displacement of people across entire continents without despair? How was it the fate of her generation to be in the front line of this dystopian nightmare? So arriving at Cambridge University had been a shock. Like finding herself amongst a massed

gathering of sleep-walking lemmings. 'Wake up,' she'd wanted to shout when her attempts to discuss environmentalism were met only with blank-eyed indifference. 'You're meant to be the brightest and the best. Can't you see your planet needs you!' Every aspect of her fellow students' lives, their Easter ski trips, the fast food they consumed, the luxury internet packages piled up awaiting collection in the porter's lodge – did no one care about the cost to the Earth? And the answer was self-evident – the brightest and the best wanted what they wanted and they wanted it now. Just like everyone else. Even in the well-preserved echelons of a heritage city like Cambridge, there was a continual febrile rumble of cranes and building work at its peripheries, making it impossible not to be continually aware of man's compulsive drive towards perpetual expansion and consumption.

In time she began to meet like-minded people with common concerns and that had helped. It had been invigorating to find herself part of a group consciousness so determined to demolish the internalised biases and blind spots of the old order. Together they were a social movement to be reckoned with. No undertones of gender or racial bias were allowed to slip beneath their radar. They shared a common and unassailable commitment to try to halt the relentless assault of capitalism on the world's increasingly fragile resources. She and her fellow activists were the upholders of natural justice, rising in her mind's eye like Themis, the Greek goddess of Justice and Law, to hold aloft the scales of impartiality in one hand and the sword of people power in the other. She had left university without a backward glance to live on caffeine and cigarettes and work as a full-time activist.

Around the next corner, she was startled to come upon a man sweeping the ground with a dried palm frond. Curious, she drew closer, taking in what appeared to be a rudimentary open-air kitchen he had constructed, complete with a rusting camping stove and a large plastic container of water, next to it a circle of boulders that served as chairs and a table. The man nodded a greeting as she came abreast of him. He was burnt a deep umber by the sun and his head was shaved, apart from a small plait at the nape of his neck and a goatee beard that bristled like a washing-up brush from his chin.

'Hey there.'

'Hola.'

He poured her some water from the plastic container, which she drank in deep gulps as she surveyed his possessions laid out with such care under the sun.

'You live here?'

He nodded. He pointed to a deep vertical fissure above them in the cliff face. 'Up there is bedroom. I was once pop star in Czech Republic. Gold records, money, everything very nice,' he said. 'But now I am full-time member of resistance movement.'

She wondered if she had heard him correctly. 'The resistance movement?'

He leant forward and said something *sotto voce* she couldn't quite catch. He glanced over his shoulder and leant closer still.

'I am specialist in Deep State, but my colleagues and me – we monitor chem-trails and 5G too,' he said before tapping his finger against his nose. 'We are waiting. When everything collapses, rest assured we will mobilise. It won't be long now . . .'

His eyes burnt with a fierce zealotry and she felt how her sceptical smile must mirror the sceptical smiles that William and his guests had cast upon her at dinner only the night before. Her spirits sagged. She thought about asking for directions to the sea but he had already turned his back and resumed his sweeping. So she only thanked him for the water and set off again, eager to put distance between them.

As the afternoon wore on, the sea would often appear in the far distance but almost at once the track would coil away from the coast again, distance and proximity proving to be an unfolding optical illusion in this intricately twisting landscape. The terrain continually rose and fell, one hidden valley giving way to another as she ascended and descended each new mountain on the dusty trails worn by generations of shepherds and their flocks.

It was late afternoon when she came upon a camper van parked in the shade of a huge carob tree. Decorated with graffiti, all its doors were thrown open to the elements, scraps of fabric draped over the windows in an attempt to hold the sun's ferocity at bay. A puzzling quantity of feet emerged from the open rear doors and glancing inside she saw a tangle of semi-naked bodies – it was hard to be sure how many deeply tanned young men and women lay curled up asleep together like blind puppies, arms thrown wide. She passed a pot simmering on a fire, beside it the remnants of a meal congealing in the sun, piled up cold boxes, scattered pots and pans. Under the shade of nearby trees, a bare-chested young man was spinning poi, the trailing ribbons tracing concentric circles about his head. He paused from his exertions to nod a greeting, before taking a gulp of water and wiping away the sweat from his forehead on his arm. Every part of his exposed flesh was covered in tattoos.

'Will I reach the sea soon?' she asked in Spanish.

'All roads in Ibiza end in the sea.' His tumble of sun-bleached dreadlocks fell almost to his waist and the light caught the glitter of facial piercings. 'But stay here if you like.' He nodded at the bubbling pot. 'We make a super nice mushroom ceremony tonight.'

'Another time maybe . . .'

He lifted his shoulders – *suit yourself* – before turning back to resume his graceful arabesques. And once more on the path, the comfort of solitude soon enveloped her again. At some point she jumped when a snake slithered close to her feet, before vanishing into the undergrowth with such eerie silence and speed, she wondered if it might have been no more than a hallucination. A little later, a grouse flashed across her path, making her laugh out loud at the frantic manner in which the cluster of chicks orbited like miniature replicas about their mother.

This time, when she reached the crest of the next hill, the sliver of sea that opened up along the horizon was at last close enough that she could just make out distant boats. The view was framed by pine-covered hills on either side that dropped away into the deep cleft of yet another wooded valley. As she stood surveying the view, something thudded out of the foliage to land on her shoulder. It was a cricket, so improbably green it looked more like a self-propelling fashion accessory, its dainty antenna tickling her chin. 'Hola bichito,' she laughed. But as abruptly as it arrived, it had sprung away again.

She sat down on a rock to roll a cigarette, becoming mesmerised by a line of ants that now formed a moving convoy across the bridge of her foot as she smoked. Up close they moved in the jerky manner of a Charlie Chaplin film, construction workers hurrying fragments of twigs from one place to another, crisscrossing with foraging parties in search of food.

Once she reached the sea she would follow the coastal path south. Head to the port. Turn the whole debacle of her meeting with William into a funny story when she got back to the UK. She rose, stubbing the cigarette out with care before putting the butt in her pocket. *Turns out my biological father is an arch capitalist.* She liked how breezy that sounded. *And my wicked stepmother clearly intended to poison me.*

She took out her phone. *Hey Doll*, she texted. *Everything gone tits up. Think I might head home. Miss you. Can you talk?* But the phone made an angry buzz of refusal. Still no signal. She'd just have to figure it out by herself. Franny was twenty years older, and it was a standing joke between them that she was Alice's 'mother substitute'. Well, she'd just have to show Fran that when push came to shove, she was perfectly capable of taking care of herself. Who needed a mother? Who needed a father, come to that?

A rabbit bolted down the track, its haunches flashing white as it pivoted between hind and foreleg, before disappearing into the scrub, and all at once her heart soared and bounded with it. The world was full of people who had nothing in common with their blood relatives. Today, right now, looking out over the wide wilderness before her, she was beholden to no one. And tonight. Tonight, if necessary, she would just sleep under the stars. She was footloose and fancy free.

She stepped to the edge of the escarpment and, raising her hands to her mouth, called out across the land. The shout faded, segueing into the laughter of distant seagulls, which in turn gave way to the hum of bees amongst the flowering rosemary at her feet.

'Madam. The police are here.' Rene had to say it twice more before Cressida looked up with a start from her laptop where she was immersed in updating last-minute confirmations and cancellations.

She knew it. William had been courting mishap for years, driving far too fast. Taking those hairpin corners at his usual reckless pace. Clutching her throat, Cressida hurried to the front door with Rene at her heels. Two officers from the Guardia Civil in blue uniforms and gold epaulettes stood waiting, with their hats clamped under one arm. They might have resembled a comedy duo – the first tall and thin, the other small and round – if the guns at their hips hadn't lent them a rather more sinister aspect. A neighbour had reported the sound of hammering coming from her property, the tall one told her in rapid Spanish. Since the *Ayuntamiento* had no record of any building permit being issued to this address, they had been sent to investigate. It took a beat for her to make the change of gear. No tears necessary. Only a charm offensive. So she donned her best hostess smile, extending a hand towards the gardens, inviting them to come and take a look.

As they wove their way between the tables set out now at regular intervals across the lawn, Cressida found herself gabbling. They were preparing to celebrate her husband's fiftieth birthday, she said as they came to stand beside the tent.

'Mi marido suele decir – sólo eres mayor una vez.' *As my husband likes to say – you are only old once*, Cressida said, noting with alarm the cool manner in which the officer's eyes traversed the garden, her attempt at humour failing to raise even the ghost of a smile in either man. The smaller officer in particular was looking about with an alarming diligence. But daring to dart the briefest of glances in the direction of the illegal underground guest wing, she was relieved to find no hint of anything untoward amongst the dense growth of trees and inwardly blessed Rene for advising her to keep the camouflage nets in place even after the work was completed.

In recent years, a brisk trade in camouflage nets had sprung up on the island. Rene had got them from someone who claimed to have bought them from the Israeli army. For if the *Ayuntamiento* turned down your application for a building permit, the camouflage nets were the only way of ensuring that the work could proceed regardless.

The smaller of the two men gestured to the east. His grandfather had been born in a finca just over the way, he said in Spanish, and he had often come here as a boy when the previous Ibicenco family were in residence. His grandfather would bring him along to help with the *matanza*, the annual slaughtering of the family pig.

'All the neighbours would gather. Not one part of that pig was wasted.'

'Even the tail?'

He cracked his first smile.

'Even the tail!'

And then to Cressida's intense relief, the officers were turning back with amiable nods and smiles towards their car. It crossed her mind that they might be expecting a payment as a thank you for not making trouble. Black Money, as it was known, a phrase aptly reminiscent of the pirates who once terrorised the island. Yet she had no idea what the etiquette of offering such a thing might be.

They paused before the open door of one of the converted outhouses, where the giant screen in the cinema room had been set to a sports channel, silently relaying an international football match. The shorter policeman made a small exclamation of recognition. This had been the very corral where the pig once lived, he said, his face suffused with nostalgia. He watched the players running across the field in high definition, absorbing the changes wrought by time with a wistful nod, before walking back towards their car.

'Just make sure your guests dispose of their cigarettes safely,' the taller policeman said in Spanish. At least that's what she thought he had said. *Colillas*. Didn't that mean cigarette butts?

She nodded. 'Of course. The last thing any of us would want is a forest fire on our hands!'

The two men climbed into their car again and she bobbed her head and smiled ingratiatingly as if in lieu of payment, while the taller of the two officers acknowledged her deference with a statesman-like inclination of the head.

'Adiós!' Her smile faded as the gates closed.

She exhaled, wondering with a sinking heart if she shouldn't find Alice and try to smooth things over. But she soon thought better of it. Alice had, after all, caught her red-handed and it was impossible to know what excuse she could possibly offer in mitigation. Returning to take up her list again, she tried instead to summon a suitably soothing affirmation, but for once nothing came to mind.

Just as the last traces of light in the sky were beginning to wane, Alice came to a track whose access was blocked by a padlocked chain strung between two posts. The path ran on through the trees, before curving away and out of sight.

'Interesting,' she said out loud, to give herself courage – and, ducking under the chain, set off with a newly jaunty step. 'Let's see what's what, shall we.'

The track passed through a forest of dense pine trees so immense in stature that there was no more than the narrowest strip of sky overhead to light her way. As the setting sun backlit everything with a flaming iridescence, the air relinquished its weight, little by little becoming silken again.

At length she came to a boundary wall, her way now barred by an automated gate with a security camera attached to one of the gateposts. She pressed the buzzer and waited. Only birdsong. She waved to the camera. Still just the last huzzah of birds at dusk. She stepped back and taking hold of her bag threw it over the wall with as much propulsion as she could muster. She heard it land with a soft thud on the other side and waited, listening to the silence – one finger raised in the air. No guard dogs on the loose, then.

Taking a running jump at the gate she hung perilously for a moment by her fingertips, before pulling herself up and astride it. She found herself looking down on a gravelled courtyard and the glass-fronted façade of a modernist villa.

Through the trees a glimpse of a distant tennis court and beyond it the sun, now a great red globe, so low in the sky its dying radiance was fragmented into rosy shafts of light by the trees. The racket of cicadas ceased, as if someone had pressed a mute button, and in that moment she could smell her own sweat and view herself from afar.

You bloody idiot – what the hell are you getting yourself into now?

Then, as she had done so many times before, she gathered herself and jumped anyway.

Cressida had fixed her eyes on the floor in an attempt to hide the righteous sense of triumph that burnt in her. William took in her drawn face before coming to sit beside her, frowning as he absorbed the news.

'So Alice went for a walk and that's the last anyone saw of her?'

'Exactly. Mary saw her setting off just before lunch. One of Rene's men said she stopped and asked him the way to the sea.'

'Just before lunch . . .' he echoed in dismay. It did seem an alarmingly long time not to have heard anything. He picked up his phone and tried Alice's number but it only rang briefly before going to voicemail. Three more times in quick succession the voicemail thwarted him.

'And I can only presume, since she's taken her bag and passport, that she's not planning on coming back.' Even she could hear how unconvincing her offhand tone sounded.

His shoulders sagged. Perhaps he should try to track down her father, he said. He couldn't think of anyone else he might know who was connected with her. Now he came to think about it, it was extraordinary how little they still knew about Alice.

'Luckily, nothing else seems to be missing. So far as we can tell anyway.' The words had slipped from her, just like that. They looked at each other. No undoing them now.

'What on earth is that supposed to mean?'

She held out the piece of paper. 'Well, she's obviously in some kind of trouble with the police. Mary found this folded inside one of her books.'

Cressida watched William scan it several times. It was a bail slip issued to Alice by the Nottinghamshire Constabulary. She was required to appear in court in a fortnight's time.

'For Christ's sake, Cressida. This is hardly evidence my daughter might be a thief . . .'

He sprang to his feet again, his tone remaining more incredulous than angry, though the proprietorial inflexion with which he had infused '*my daughter*' caught her a body blow. The instinct to land a counterpunch flashed through her at such speed the words formed themselves again as if of their own volition.

'Well, you might be interested to know that I checked her date of birth in her passport before she left – and there it was in black and white. Just as I thought. You cheated on me.'

He stood winded, before wheeling on his heel, and slamming the door behind him. No one could blame Cressida for making investigations of her own when he persisted in lying through his teeth. She jutted her chin, as if in defiance of an imagined accuser. She challenged any reasonable person not to have done the same.

From the kitchen came the rhythmic sound of the chef chopping. It was time to go and change for dinner. She stepped into the sitting-room, where all the clutter of the day had already been tidied away by Mary, and out of sheer habit moved about checking for any oversights. She'd heard the guests returning from their boat trip at least an hour ago. But none of them were anywhere to be seen yet, doubtless busy showering in their rooms as they chatted companionably to their partners or stretched out on their beds catching up on messages. From upstairs came the sound of the children being given their bath, a joyful crescendo of laughter from Joe followed by Mary's gentle teasing. She stood very still, listening to the intimate off-stage bustle of family life.

As usual, the unopened emails had filled up William's in-tray again like rapacious weeds. In the hope of distracting himself, he fired back a few answers to the easy ones, before deciding to leave the remainder for later. Then he opened up a new page on his computer screen, which he labelled *On Turning 50*. But as the sting of Cressida's righteous indignation receded, an unease about Alice's disappearance rose up in its stead. *Where in God's name could she have got to?* William poured a generous whisky to steady himself, before sitting down at his computer. There were no messages from Alice anywhere. He tapped out a speedy WhatsApp.

Hey! Worried about you. All ok? Hoping to see you for dinner at 8.

He rose from his desk and went over to examine the architect's model. Thirty luxury villas rendered in balsa wood. He had been intending to show it to Alice on his return. Had planned to explain how much care had been taken to site each villa discreetly in the landscape and how the architects had proposed a state-of-the-art geothermal energy system. It was true William had knocked the idea on the head – but it occurred to him now he might have been too hasty. Perhaps he could tell her about his change of heart. *You've already made me reconsider a few things, you know.* The phrase *Eco Thoughtful* came to him and he jotted it down, making a mental note to get it added to the sales documents. It was true he couldn't claim to be entirely up to speed on these things. But that was why he paid people who were.

Moving on, he paused to glance over the piles of glossy new sales brochures that had just come back from the printer's. *The 30 luxury villas are located in a gated compound with air conditioning, 24 hour manned security, gym, spa, garden irrigation system and automated home management set-up. All properties come with access to a private helipad.* You can't halt progress, Alice, he had intended to say in a light-hearted manner that didn't sound too glib. Like it or not, the wheels must keep on turning. Progress is the lifeblood of this island. Her idealism was undeniably charming. Jess, of course, had also had the same propensity to be high-minded. There were certain principles she'd held to be inviolate and there was no reasoning with her on them.

Yet Alice had barely known her mother. He frowned. The most likely scenario was that Alice had gone off on some youthful adventure somewhere. She struck him as a resourceful young woman, only too capable of taking care of herself. She'd be back soon enough.

He helped himself to another generous slug of whisky. It had been a serious miscalculation on his part to assume Alice wouldn't be aware of the circumstances of her conception. Jess had obviously told her husband everything. And he in turn had, after all these years, made a clean breast to Alice. So now Cressida's suspicions had been validated she would continue to seethe until everyone had gone home. And then? And then – the marital gloves would be off.

He tapped his desk with an agitated finger, recalling the conversation with Alice as they'd stood beside the well. Could the island's water supply really be running out? He'd certainly heard that a number of the aquifers in the south had already run dry.

Though he had never confided this to anyone, one of the things that had first appealed to him about relocating to Ibiza was that it appeared to be a good place to keep his family safe from the myriad threats to their future health and well-being that so haunted the daily news: the floods, pandemics and terrorist bombs. He'd even checked their height above sea level – and invested a significant amount in a combination of Bitcoins and gold bullion that he hoped might cover all unforeseen eventualities. (Several bars of gold bullion were now stacked in the safe. Fearing it might unnerve Cressida to expound on its potential usefulness in the event of an apocalypse, he had offered instead a fictitious account of a Saudi Arabian client who preferred to pay him in this way.) *But what good were Bitcoins and gold bullion if the island's water supply dried up?*

He went back to his desk and clicked a few times in search of new distractions. The international property investments website showed the interior of a well-appointed log cabin, through its picture window a spectacular view of snowy mountain peaks. *This June, Christie's International Real Estate brings you a special selection of estates fresh to market.* In the foreground, someone had set up a single armchair next to a side table, on which was set a large glass of red wine. It wasn't too hard to imagine inserting himself sipping wine while surveying the magnificence of the scenery at the end of a hard day's off-piste skiing. So what on earth was he doing living on this small dry island in the Balearics, he wondered disconsolately, when he could be living this other, finer life in Switzerland? Wasn't a country with such boundless quantities of groundwater precisely the kind of place that a man with a young family should have settled?

At 7 p.m. precisely, the conference call came through. Three peevish financiers in three different countries gathering for an update on the slow progress of the Cala Conta project.

William listened as his project manager did her usual impeccable job. She had finally got access to *the* key *funcionarios* in the relevant department, she was assuring the investors in soothing tones. And it looked as if a discreet sweetener was all it should take to smooth the way forward. But the fact that so little was required of William allowed the thought of the dwindling water supply to keep intruding. He continued to utter the odd *uh-huh* of assent while turning back to seek solace amongst the jewel-like images on the Christie's website. Clicking on one of the links, he found a world of properties curated according to hobby: estates for wine lovers in France, chalets for sports enthusiasts in Aspen. Whole possibilities of other lives like lights in darkened rooms snapping on. By twists and turns he found himself on the website of a fifteen-storey luxury apartment complex built in an underground Atlas missile silo in Kansas. *Solutions for Survival Living. Act now because this is a VERY limited opportunity to get total 'life assurance' for you and your family in the event of just about any major crisis.* As the conference call rumbled interminably on in his earpiece, he stared into space, trying to envisage the four of them safely tucked up in an underground missile silo with video screens of countryside intended to substitute for the real views that would no longer be any more than a distant memory.

Alice scaled the drystone wall that abutted the house without too much difficulty, the gaps between the rocks offering generous footholds. From there, by seizing sturdy enough fistfuls of wisteria, she began to haul herself up the side of the building. Smaller branches kept breaking off, but a few of the larger ones held for just long enough to allow her to keep rising until, with a final effort of will, she drew level with the flat roof of the first floor.

After some determined jiggling, Alice managed to loosen the bolt on one of the rustier skylights and flipped it open before sitting on the frame and dropping to the floor below, falling to her knees and then onto her side, like a parachutist making an emergency landing. A quick audit of limbs established that nothing was broken and, rising to her feet, she found herself in a large open plan room with a high mezzanine stairwell that opened onto the ground floor below. Everything was in shades of white: the marble floors, the leather sofas, all as impersonal as a dentist's waiting room.

The walls were hung with giant photographs of women dressed in tiny thongs, displaying their long gleaming limbs and augmented shiny breasts.

Whoever had been staying here must have departed very recently, leaving the place in chaos. Though the kitchen had been tidied, the inhabitants appeared to have partied long after the chef headed home, for there were half-filled wine and shot glasses everywhere, overflowing ashtrays and a faint scattering of white powder on a large mirror that had been taken off a hook on the wall. Empty champagne and vodka bottles stood stacked up by the bin and the vast double fridge was filled with remnants of the previous night's dinner. Alice swung the fridge door to and fro, circulating the chill of its interior against her bare skin, as she wondered what she could eat. A sudden ravenous hunger made her all at once light-headed and she scooped dollops of hummus into her mouth, before draining a jar of olives. The coffee pot on the stove still held a faint memory of heat. The inhabitants must have slept the excesses of the night off before rising in the afternoon to depart for the airport, fuelled by a hasty shot of caffeine.

She slid open the glass doors that gave onto a spectacularly scaled pool with formal rows of espaliered olive trees planted like military sentinels. Now the sun was gone, the pool had become a rectangle of gleaming, shifting mercury. Beyond it a bar and an empty jacuzzi with rows of sunloungers facing out over distant views of the *campo*. Nearby, a giant statue of Buddha towering several metres high sat cross-legged – his eyes closed and his open palm raised as if to hold the hedonism of his setting at bay.

She shed her clothes and dived in, gliding to the far end in one long sweep before settling into a strong stroke. She swam until she had erased all thought, and when she was done, it was dark. The automatic lighting system had transformed the garden, theatrically lit trees punctuating the darkness, intensifying the shrouded boundaries at the peripheries. Bats darted and dipped across the pool as the moon rose from behind the trees.

She climbed out, water streaming from her, a question, like a flashlight popping. *What if Pete was mistaken? What proof had anyone offered that William really was her biological father?* She exhaled. *Oh God. What if she'd gone storming in like some human wrecking ball when someone, somewhere had simply got their wires crossed?* Jess had told Pete that William was the father. That much was true. And Pete had obviously always unquestioningly accepted what Jess told him. Why would he not? William too had been surprisingly and perhaps gallantly ready to accept his paternity. But maybe her mother had been mistaken. Or had an agenda they could only guess at now. She had a sudden urge to talk this over with Franny. She was always such a good sounding board for life's conundrums. But when she picked up her phone, she found there was still no signal and that her text message to Franny remained unsent, a red exclamation mark beside it.

She walked back into the house, leaving a trail of wet footprints. On one of the strewn coffee tables was a mirrored box. Inside, amongst an assortment of pills and powders, she found a lump of hash and, hooking out papers and a roach, sat down to roll herself a joint. At the press of one of the remote controls, music boomed through the ceiling speakers and, still damp from her swim, she began to dance as she smoked it – wagging her index fingers in the air before drumming them against her ribcage and strutting about like a bandy-legged rooster. She sometimes made Fran laugh by dancing like this. But tonight she had only herself to amuse.

She danced as only someone free of eyes upon them can, and once she fell back onto one of the giant sofas, she began to laugh, crossing her arms about her body, hugging her amusement to herself.

How could you ever have doubted Pete was your father?

'Because he sounded so certain.'

She raised her palms to the skies in remonstration.

Well, get them both to do a DNA test, then, you nutter.

The ripple of the music moved through her, commanding her to rise to her feet again, and she moved with a joyful abandon until a wave of exhaustion knocked her sideways. Bumping along the walls, she found herself in the long corridor. Opening doors at random, she discovered a gym, a spa and then a small windowless room that housed a bank of blank security monitors. Wandering further, she came to another long corridor, off which were a series of bedrooms in disarray. The master bedroom featured a floor-to-ceiling metal pole at its centre. The satin sheets were strewn about the bed, their shiny twists duplicated in the vast ceiling mirror above. Beyond the bed was a bath so big it was more a plunge pool, with crumpled black towels and empty silver capsules scattered about it. Repelled by the faint animal scent of the room, she stumbled back into the corridor again. Every door she opened revealed another bedroom in disarray, until she finally came to one that was untouched. She had barely lain down before she had fallen into a deep and dreamless sleep.

At dinner that night, Alice's absence was the main topic of conversation. No sooner had she appeared as if from nowhere than she was gone again! There was much speculation about which of the island's many seductions could have lured her. Much agreement that she knew how to take care of herself.

'I mean, she's hardly the shrinking violet type,' Marcus said, looking about the table.

'But the whole thing is just so inexplicable. I've rung and rung. Left countless messages . . .' William gestured with his fork.

'Trust me. She will have bumped into someone who's invited her to one of those illegal trance nights. Or a secret sweat lodge somewhere deep in the forest – you know what this island's like – and there she'll be, having the time of her life.' Kate patted William's hand. 'She'll be back.'

Cressida surveyed the table with a tremulous smile that conveyed a faint if forlorn trace of genuine hope. 'You know, I can't help thinking that it's almost as if we just invented her.'

3

William was showering, when he caught the thin top note of his mobile ringtone over the thunder of water. Having slept fitfully, he had woken at dawn with a leaden apprehension, which only escalated after he hurried to Alice's room and found her bed still neatly made, ready to receive an occupant who had never returned. No sooner had he registered the ringtone than he was scrabbling for a towel and hurrying across the bedroom in a cascade of soapy water, only to discover that he had a missed call from Alice. He rang her back at once, his heart leaping in relief when she picked up on the second ring.

'Alice! Alice – are you . . . ? Is everything . . . ?'

But the quality of the line was so poor and Alice was talking across him with such rapidity, it took a while to make sense of what she was saying. He caught something about getting lost. Then something about having had to spend the night in an empty villa. Yet her tone was elated. Not the voice of someone in trouble but of someone on a great adventure. No, she hadn't the foggiest idea where she was, she said in answer to the question he had attempted to pose several times before she finally heard it. Her words came with abrupt auditory clarity now he had gone out onto the balcony in search of better reception.

'But there's absolutely no need to worry. Now I've got this far, I've decided to just keep on going.'

'Keep on going?' he repeated, the soapsuds stinging his eyes like pepper. The words were shorn of meaning. 'Going where? For God's sake, Alice. You've only just got here!'

'It's all a bit mad, I know. But I'm going to head home. Leave you guys in peace.'

'Woah. Alice. Send me a pin and I'll come and find you. Let's talk this through, face to face, in a civilised fashion.'

What on earth had he been thinking? Why had he not cleared his diary when she first appeared so miraculously like that? All that prevarication and doubt about what he could and should be telling her and now, without warning, she had seized the initiative and fled.

'I'll be there,' he cried, when the pin arrived and he saw it was hovering in the middle of a densely wooded area some distance away to the north-east. He couldn't for the life of him imagine how she had landed up there. 'I'm coming now. Stay right where you are.'

As he talked, he was struggling to pull on a pair of shorts and a T-shirt with his spare hand without taking the phone from his ear, as if she would remain attached by a virtual umbilical cord as long as he could keep this audio connection open between them. But she had already cut the line. He snatched up his watch, a wad of cash and his car keys from the side table; the barest essentials, he hoped in his blind panic, of a man on a rescue mission. On an afterthought he ran back for his sunglasses. *The symbol of new ideas and courageous self-expression reborn as wearable tech.*

Cressida was on the phone as William bolted past her for the car, throwing Alice's name over one shoulder in response to her mimed enquiry about where he was off to in such a hurry. *Found Alice*, he mouthed when she looked blank.

'What!' She took the phone from her ear, gaping in surprise.

'I'll text you with an update,' he cried as he climbed into the jeep and swung it round to face the automated gates, jabbing with savage impatience at the remote control. 'We should be back in an hour or so.' He was halfway down the drive when his way was blocked yet again by an oncoming lorry with a row of portable lavatories stacked on the back, and he cursed under his breath as he waited impatiently for it to laboriously reverse until there was sufficient space to pass. But no sooner had he darted round it than his way was blocked again by a wine merchant's van that had thundered around the corner before coming to an abrupt halt in a cloud of dust in front of him. The driver wound down his window to ask in broken English if this was the right way to the house having the big party tonight – but instead of answering, William only flung up his hands in exasperation before navigating around the van by swinging the wheel sideways to mount a steep bank of tangled undergrowth and thump down on the far side.

Getting to the area was easy enough, but after that, though he took the main road heading west from the church as the pin indicated, then not long afterwards the tricky series of minor turns it proposed, he was soon in a warren of diverging tracks too numerous and intricate for the pin to replicate, and then the signal abruptly vanished. As the jeep bumped and bucked over the potholes, he scanned the passing *campo* with growing desperation but there was no sign anywhere of a dwelling that could have offered Alice shelter for the night. Every time he checked his phone it only confirmed that there was still no reception, and at some point he held it up – like someone face to face with their mortal enemy – and swore at it, speckling its glass front with spittle. Later still, when he realised he was more hopelessly lost than ever, he even struck the steering wheel with his fists. *What if he couldn't find her and she sat waiting for him all day? Worse still – what if she tired of waiting and set off on foot as she had sounded so impatient to do?* At last, delirious with rage and navigating in a reckless fashion he only hoped threw two fingers to the fuckers in charge, he happened to arrive at a track whose way was blocked by the padlocked chain, just as she had described.

He abandoned the car beside the chain and, stepping over it, set off at a fast trot, sweating and swearing as he hurried down the long track that wound its way through the forest. So much for his foolish joke about missing all the early trials and tribulations of fatherhood. This was a baptism of fire indeed! The sun had dried the surface of the track to a fine chalk powder that rose in clouds at every step to dust the vast trees on either side a ghostly white, giving the impression that despite the clammy heat, they were laden with snow. Even as he hurried, he was dimly struck by the unnerving feeling he was leaving the known world behind.

Rounding a curve in the track, he saw ahead the boundary wall of the villa and there, sitting with her back against the gatepost, was a visibly restive Alice.

'What on earth's going on?' he called, striving for a jocular tone as he strode towards her. 'You've been on the island for twenty-four hours and now you're off again! Was it something I said?'

She rose with a truculent air, her backpack cradled in her arms, and came to a halt a few feet away. They stood, both at a loss as to how to proceed.

'I only rang to let you know I was OK. I didn't mean for you to come rushing over.' Her tone was cool.

'So you broke into this villa last night?'

She shrugged dismissively. 'It was either that or sleep under a carob tree . . . Anyway, the whole place was trashed. No way anyone will have a clue I was ever there.'

She looked remarkably fresh this morning, he thought, torn between relief and exasperation. More than fresh – she was gleaming with a steely resolve, as if some inner light had been lit within.

As they walked back in the direction of the car, she spoke with a calm authority. 'Once I get to the sea, I'll just follow the coastal path south until I reach the port. It shouldn't take long. And at the port I'll catch a ferry to Barcelona. And from Barcelona a train.' Her open-palmed gesture illustrated the beautiful simplicity of her plan. 'Better for you guys to have one less guest to worry about.' She hesitated. 'I don't know if Cressida said anything but we had a bit of a falling-out yesterday. I found her going through my things . . .'

'Look – don't worry about Cressida. She's just stressed about the party. Once the whole thing gets going, she'll be right as rain. Why not come home with me. Have a swim. Grab some lunch. And if the prospect of the party still doesn't light your fire, well Rene can always just drop you off wherever it is you want to . . .'

But she was already shaking her head. He tried again. 'Alice. No one in their right mind would choose to be out walking in heat like this.'

She only stepped back, hugging her bag to her as if to ward off his lobbying.

'OK. If you really want to go, then fine – that's fine – I'll just drive you to the port myself. It'll take no time in the car.'

She showed him the drinking water and dried almonds she had packed. 'The sea's so close now.' She pointed to the west. 'Literally just on the other side of those mountains. I love to walk. It'll be an adventure. Do me good.'

She slung the bag on her back, and hooked her thumbs

through the straps, clearly restless to be on her way, and he was assailed by this curious awareness of the root connection between them, countered so perplexingly by being at one and the same time such perfect strangers.

They took it in turns to duck under the padlocked chain and came to stand beside the jeep, whose engine was still clicking as it cooled and retracted. He glanced at his phone, making a quick mental audit of his schedule for the day. A faint resumption of signal had brought a flood of messages. He recalled the myriad party details yet to be finalised. Not least his speech. An incoming text message flashed up on the screen, the phone briefly pulsating like a living creature in his hand.

'It's Cressida – asking if you're OK.' He tapped out a quick response, his fingers dancing over the keyboard as the screen reflected his perspiring face back at him.

Long story – just trying to work things out – call you in 5.

After a short pause, the phone buzzed again. 'Cressida says . . .' His voice trailed away as he read on. *Bollocks to your cock and bull stories.* He exhaled. Jesus. He looked again at Alice, poised with such impatience as the morning sun made a perfect halo of light about her head. Beyond her the path bent and twisted, the rising heat releasing the scent of thyme and from somewhere that faint perfume of curry powder that so often haunted the undergrowth.

'So I really can't persuade you to come back with me, then?'

She nodded. 'Nope. You really, definitely can't.'

He made a few more quick calculations. She was right. The sea couldn't be so far away. And when all was said and done, what greater priority could he have than seeing his long-lost daughter safely on her way? He was hardly going to just drive home and abandon her out here in the wilderness.

'OK. Then I'll walk with you just until you reach the coastal path.'

'Honestly, no need. I'll be fine.'

He checked his watch with the decisive flourish of a man who has resolved on a course of action from which he is not about to be deflected.

'Well, I'm afraid I'm going to insist. I'd hate you to think you had a monopoly on being stubborn. I'd never forgive myself if you got lost again.'

They stood assessing one another. Then she abruptly spun on her heel and started off down the path.

'Suit yourself,' she said, without looking back.

He was turning to hasten after her, when he became conscious of the weight of the car keys in his hand, and went back again to hide them under one of the wheel hubs. As he set off, he was surprised to note a new buoyancy in his step, as if a slender air pocket of helium had inflated between his foot and sandal.

'To be honest it's a relief to get away from all the mayhem for a bit. Stretch the old legs,' he said, dabbing at his forehead with the hem of his T-shirt once he managed to catch up with her.

The ochre earth of the track had been churned by winter rains into deep gullies that were now baked into rock-hard craters. It was not so much a path as the dried-out belly of a winter *torrente*, William realised, his expensive sandals slipping on its ceramic-like sheen as he struggled to keep up with her.

'What will you do for lunch?' he called at her departing back when she had soon outpaced him again.

'Dunno. Just thought I'd go with the flow, I guess. Not something that comes naturally to you, I suspect.'

'No,' William conceded. 'Never had the foggiest idea how to flow.' After a few more attempts at jocular gambits fell on stony ground, he began to lose heart and they walked for a while in silence.

'I must say, listening to you the other night,' he tried again when the silence had grown too oppressive to bear. 'I thought your commitment to environmental issues was pretty impressive.'

'Really?' She sounded genuinely surprised, glancing at him as if to check he wasn't mocking her. 'I'm always beating myself up for not doing more. My goal is zero-waste living.'

'Zero-waste living?'

She shrugged. 'I try to only buy what I need. And even then, nothing pre-packaged. So, I wash my hair in vinegar. Brush my teeth with a compostable toothbrush and baking soda. Just basic stuff like that.'

'Brush your teeth with baking soda!' William repeated, pulling an involuntary face of distaste. 'Bloody hell, Alice.'

Perhaps every new generation required some kind of existential threat to cut their ideological teeth on. Hadn't his own grown up in the shadow of the nuclear bomb? He wondered whether to float the idea – but fearing she might take offence at the implication her environmental concerns were no more than a passing symptom of her youth, he decided it would be wiser to steer into less contentious waters.

'And what's your father up to these days?'

'Oh, same old, same old. Dad's still a fine art photographer,' Alice said, appropriating the noun without any apparent unease about its potential complexity. 'But of course it's not the easiest way to make a living. So he often has to take on crap jobs just to pay the bills.'

William gestured at her to take a turning onto a new track and they began to wind their way uphill again.

'We moved about a lot when I was little. He always had this insatiable curiosity to see the world. And so we lived in all sorts of weird and wonderful places. His way of dealing with the loneliness after Mum died, I guess. But as I grew up we became a tight team. We were each other's everything.'

'I'm very glad to hear that,' William said, making an effort to sound pleased. Indeed was pleased. Relieved beyond measure. Yet somehow her fond descriptions of life with Pete also caused an unsettling complexity of emotion to arise in him.

Recalling something, she began to laugh. 'Can you believe he once spent two months working as Father Christmas in

Winter Wonderland just so he could take me to Cuba? He'd always promised me a trip there for my sixteenth birthday and he was going to honour that promise come hell or high water.'

Her laughter was imbued with the amused tenderness people employ when recalling the foibles of someone particularly dear to them. She glanced at him to assess his response, as if daring him to betray some kind of judgement.

'It must have been quite a shock. To just be told out of the blue that Pete wasn't actually your biological father.'

'It was like, Pqqqqq!' She mimed the shape of an explosion breaking about her head. She cast about for words, her hands grasping at air. 'It's really hard to describe. I guess it was like I'd never had a mother and now all of a sudden I didn't even have a father.'

He had no idea what he could possibly say that might comfort her.

'But. I've been thinking. You know. Wondering. We should probably get a DNA test, shouldn't we?'

'We should.'

'So you'd be up for that?' She sounded relieved.

'Of course. If we can ever actually get back to civilisation again . . .' He patted his pocket to retrieve his phone. No phone. He patted the other pocket, before it came to him in a panic-stricken revelation that he had left it sitting in its satnav holder in the car. 'Don't suppose you're able to get Google maps up are you?'

She held up her phone to show there was still no signal. He looked at his watch and did a quick mental tally. Still plenty of time. They would just have to work this through logically, step by step. He cupped his hands to his mouth and called out across the land. 'Hellooooo. Hellooooo.' Not even an echo. Two *Homo sapiens*. Alone in the wilderness. Two *Homo sapiens* who had inexplicably slipped through a crack in their own lives.

He felt the press of sun against his bowed neck as he walked, every now and then plucking away his T-shirt, which had stuck to his abdomen like damp cling wrap. Feeling all at once overwhelmed, he sat down on a rock and dried his face with his T-shirt. Alice handed him her water bottle and he took it gratefully, drinking in noisy gulps.

'I did tell you not to come,' she said, snatching the water bottle back as she set off down the path again, swinging her arms in a defiant display of undimmed spirit.

William rose to follow her. She was right. He had only himself to blame. But it was surely just a matter of time now until they came upon a house. And when they did, he would knock on the door and ask to borrow a phone. One call was all it would take and Rene would be on his way.

At the top of the next mountain, the views opened up to reveal a vast new valley that stretched away as far as the eye could see, the tree canopy so dense they might have been looking over the Amazon rainforest. It was quite extraordinary how different everything looked once one left the familiar highways and byways, he thought in despair. And though he scanned the wide panorama, there was not a hint of human habitation anywhere to be seen.

She'd announced the event months ago, with some half-cocked conviction it would remain forever an abstract – and the next thing she knew the day was rudely rushing at her, despite the fact there were still a million things to do. Now her husband had vanished into thin air just hours before the very event that was intended to be dedicated not only to him but to the marvellous family they had created together. And the whole front of house had anyway already been publicly shattered by the surprise arrival and shortly thereafter even more surprising disappearance of her husband's illegitimate daughter. A daughter who she had now learnt – despite all reassurances to the contrary – was conceived in an act of flagrant infidelity in the early days of their relationship. The memory of William's betrayal seared and scalded her all over again. It couldn't have been long after his infidelity that she had found the newspaper cutting about Jess secreted in William's wallet. The article celebrated Jess's work support-ing an education programme for women in Afghanistan and was illustrated with a fetching photograph of her looking maddeningly intrepid in a jeep. Cressida had confiscated the cutting. Still had it somewhere amongst her papers. *Know*

thine enemy. She had gazed at the photograph in low moments, searching Jess's smiling face and hating this woman who had succeeded in capturing William's heart in a way she knew perfectly well she had never done.

Later she saw Jess's obituary and heard William's friends discussing her death. Had watched him sink into a dark place, though he said not a word to her. In a funny way the death of her rival only made it harder. Impossible to combat the sanctity that untimely death bequeathes upon the departed. And then. Then the whole thing had over time receded into the background of their lives, until that first detonation just a few months ago: the astounding news that Jess and William had had a child together – that this illegitimate child had now come of age and wanted to meet. And then her unexpected appearance in their very midst. A second and rather more public detonation.

Cressida sighed. And what on earth was she meant to make of that cryptic text message from William? Why did his phone just continually go through to voicemail? If in her secret heart of hearts, she had hoped that these elaborate birthday preparations might somehow remedy the ever deepening disconnect between them, it was dispiriting to have to acknowledge that somehow the exact converse was occurring.

She took up her phone to skim through her Instagram feed in search of distraction. Someone she barely knew doing a star jump off the deck of a beautiful boat – caught just before they hit the water. *Can life get any better!* someone had written beneath a picture of themselves standing at the peak of a mountain with arms raised in triumph. An advertisement moved across the screen. *Sensational news. We've found the dress of your dreams. The dress you'll love for ever.* Then hard on its heels an unsolicited news headline. *Four million people flee Venezuela in mass exodus of despair.*

That strange sensation came again, as if Cressida had swallowed a moth that was intent on liberation. So many workers were now coming and going that those who wanted to leave were having to step to one side of the path to make way for those who had just arrived. No sign as yet of the flower delivery lady. Nor the bar staff on whose elevating services the entire success of the evening rested. She'd already had one disappointment. Instead of the one hundred freshly caught lobster she'd ordered from a local fisherman, she'd received only a curt text, *No es posible entregar la langosta.* Well, she certainly wouldn't be recommending his services to anyone. She deleted his details from her database.

She double tapped on various Instagram posts, her despondency growing, as if each 'like' only marked a descent in spirits. Then, in an attempt to rally, she uploaded a photograph onto her own account of the children looking adorable as they stood in front of the Moroccan marquee. *Beyond excited about tonight's festivities for my darling husband,* she typed. *Living the dream! @familyGifford.* Hearing a hoot at the gate, Cressida hurried outside – and there was the DJ arriving in good time to begin setting up. There might still be no darling husband but at least there would be music. Close behind him the water truck on its third trip of the day, followed moments later by the familiar hissing and sighing of its undercarriage as it backed into the courtyard to begin decanting its cargo into the *cisterna*.

However luxuriously well-appointed the front of house might appear, behind the scenes, life in the sought-after country houses of Ibiza was little more than high-class camping. So while lavish house parties were a familiar feature of island life, they could also prove something of a logistical high-wire act.

But at least their house guests had been successfully dispatched for the day. A boozy lunch at a fashionable beach club on the salt plains in the south, and by the time they returned, everything would be ready for a night of partying. What was it Charlie had said? *The hostess with the mostest.* The phrase still rankled. *I was surely destined for more than this*, she thought as she separated ashtrays from their bubble wrap, unable to close down the familiar trajectory of self-castigation now it had raised its snake-like head. How had she ever let that hard-won career slip through her fingers? Such a complex web of marital compromises and concessions that had been tacitly struck along the way. The stringent demands of mothering had remorselessly pried her fingers one by one from their once limpet-like grip on her broadcasting career. Maternity leave had segued into going back part-time, which in turn made her a natural candidate to be in the front line of the first redundancies as cutbacks bit. And as her world shrank, as if by some curious law of physics, William's ongoing immersion in the cut and thrust of the larger world only continued to expand.

And then, in a reckless moment – a moment that even now could catch her a glancing blow of regret – when they were packing their things to come out here, she had given all her work clothes away to her lawyer sister, so painfully imbued were they with the lost authority of the public life she no longer had any reason to participate in.

She knew perfectly well when she arrived here that it was important not to get too bogged down in domesticity. Self-evidently, a modern woman should not be shackled to her stove. Yet so effectively had she subsequently redirected her formidable organisational skills into delegating the running of this new household that very soon she had more free time on her hands than she knew what to do with.

In the first few months of their relocation, Cressida would survey the school car park awash with willowy mothers picking up or dropping off – many dressed exactly like her in faux peasant outfits with only their iPhones betraying the fact that over half a century had passed since the school was founded to educate the growing number of hippy children on the island. And as she gazed upon the other mothers, she would try to ignore the growing worm of unease that something indefinable still eluded her. Why did this feel less like the fulfilling life she had always craved and more like one with all the old familiar shortcomings and uncertainties merely transposed to a sunnier location? Once the children were settled, she had relinquished even the school run to Rene in order, she said, to free herself to get on with other things. If only she knew what those other things might be.

She longed to do something worthwhile, but was at a loss where to begin. Inspired by the growing vogue for self-sufficiency, for a while she had kept four goats in a rush of early enthusiasm for their new pastoral life: skittish creatures in piebald shades of fawn and white whose shaggy coats she vaguely planned to make into wool one day – or perhaps learn how to make cheese from their milk – or just simply sketch them as they grazed so picturesquely beneath the olive trees. She had sent Rene out to source bells to hang about their necks, and briefly taken satisfaction in the distant tinkling. Until one morning she was awoken by the dainty dingling of bells to discover that all four goats had clambered nimbly out of their pen and into the gardens, where they had made short work of her flower beds. Rene had driven them away in the truck that very afternoon, promising to find another home for them, and she had never had the heart to ask where he had left them. The acquisition of eight chickens had proved more successful. Accompanied by the children, she had at first enjoyed taking the food scraps down to feed them and collecting any eggs. But once the novelty waned, it was Mary who collected the eggs and Rene who made sure the chickens had enough grain and water, and sometimes she disappointed herself by experiencing a little shudder of revulsion when one of the eggs arrived in their pretty basket soiled by a smudge of dried chicken excrement into which a rogue feather or a bit of straw had embedded itself.

For a while she toyed with setting up an amusing blog about life in Ibiza – *Baleariac Bliss* was one of the working titles – or busying herself with something charitable – though those in need of philanthropy on the island soon proved to be disappointingly thin on the ground. She did however discover that there was a food bank during the winter for the large number of people thrown into unemployment at the end of the tourist season. Yet somehow a year had come and gone and she had yet to make even a preliminary call to investigate how she might usefully contribute.

In the early days, Cressida had been delighted to learn the story of the goddess Tanit. Brought to Ibiza by the Carthaginians, Tanit was reputed to give the island a unique feminine energy. It was often said that women who moved here would flourish and frequently rid themselves of their partner in the process. She had always relished the story of the Ibicenco women. Traditionally, the sons of the family had been given the fertile inland pastures where crops could grow in abundance, while the daughters received only the barren coastal land because it served no useful purpose. So once the tourist boom came, it was the daughters who turned out to be sitting on a gold mine. She hung on to the hope that it could surely be no more than a matter of time before inspiration about what to do with her life was finally brought to her on the island's oestrogen-infused winds. But two years had passed and still she waited.

Mary was sweeping around the cluster of workers who were hanging festoon lighting, and Cressida had to hastily sidestep the little pile of fallen leaves she had gathered.

'Oopsy,' Cressida smiled at her. 'Look. You missed one.' To her surprise, Mary offered a ready smile in response as Cressida lifted up the chair so Mary could whisk her broom underneath. In the past few weeks Cressida had been pleased to feel a little warmth spark between them after what had felt a long period of subterranean attrition; Cressida wanting things done her way and Mary conceding with a faintly truculent air. *Contrary Mary.* If there were times Cressida felt bolstered by the authority Mary and Rene's stubborn adherence to deference bestowed on her, there were many other times when she felt diminished by the mysterious symbiosis of their marriage, which only served as a melancholy reminder of her own essentially solitary state.

A shrill screech made her spin about in time to see the children come running full pelt between the newly erected tables and chairs, Joe howling in terror for someone to save him, the remnants of the torn snakeskin trailing from one hand. Cressida watched in dismay as Lola fell upon him, beating him with her little fists before wrenching out a large clump of his hair, at which his squawks became an ear-splitting howl.

'Don't worry. I take them to beach,' Mary offered at once, as she hastened forward to separate the warring children and draw Joe into her arms, wiping away his tears and offering a tender kiss. 'We have lunch there. Give you space to get ready. You relax madam.'

William drained the last of the water. The sun was at its highest point now and the shadows shortened. He thought of Columbus, who didn't know where he was going when he set out – and didn't know where he had been when he got back. But at least the man had had a compass. Who in their right mind would ever have thought it a good idea to set off in the heat of summer without so much as a map to navigate by? If they collapsed in the fire of this pitiless June day, there would be no one in this great wilderness to help. Joe and Lola would grow old and never know what had become of their father. Perhaps their disappearance might merit a small item in the newspapers. *Concerns grow for missing British father and daughter.* How soon would it be before they simply lay down and gave up? Before their bones bleached and powdered to dust? Yet this could all be resolved so quickly if they could only find a road! Was a nice tarmacked bit of road that would lead them back to civilisation really too much to ask for? Or a house. Or a walker who might direct them.

Alice handed him her phone. 'Look, look. A signal.' His fingers flew to tap out the number. A long silence and then at last, a ring tone. And someone picking up. 'Hello!'

'Hello?'

'Cressida. Thank God. Look – we've got ourselves in a little bit of a . . .'

'Hello? HELLO! William? Are you . . .?'

And then the line went dead.

'Jesus.'

He dialled again. Nothing. Again. Nothing. The battery now showed such a tiny sliver of red that he tapped in a panic on the location icon. If he could just send out an SOS marking their position before the last of the battery emptied, there was still hope. On the screen, a little wheel span in slowly diminishing circles. Round and round it went. And then. Blackness. A dead piece of technology in his hand. He thrust the phone back at her.

'Fuck . . .' He kept walking, blind to everything but his abject fury at having ever got himself into this mess. 'You fuckers!' he shouted at the sky.

Yet what could they do but keep on keeping on. All at once the trail vanished into a wide outcrop of boulders that banked sharply uphill and, without a word, they began the ascent, William's sandals slipping and sliding on the wide shiny flanks of stone. The sole of one of his sandals had come loose and every few steps he had to flip it back into place with an awkward manoeuvre of the foot. He checked his watch. Four hours had somehow slid through his fingers. He took off his polo shirt – *a classic yet modern styling that looks best on the deck of a yacht* – and mopped his face and neck with it. Somewhere not so far away beyond those northerly mountains was the home he had laboured to make such a perfect sanctuary, where everything was designed to facilitate maximum comfort. Somewhere in that perfect sanctuary were scores more freshly laundered polo shirts, folded and colour-coded in their glass-fronted drawers by Mary.

A sprawling carob tree had strewn the path with its wrinkled black pods and Alice stooped to retrieve one and break it open. She nibbled on a few of the seeds nestled inside before handing the remainder to William, who raised it with caution to his nose before recoiling at its peculiar scent. A little further on they passed a fig tree heavy with ripening fruit and Alice circled until she found some that were ready to pick. She offered him one to try, and this time he consented. It was still warm from the sun, and he closed his eyes to savour the revelation of its gritty sweetness, before swallowing four more in quick succession with a greedy relish.

When a lizard flashed from the undergrowth as sinuous and swift as the coil of a whip, Alice beckoned William to come and examine the gap in the rocks where it had vanished and, bending cautiously, he was startled to discover that he and the lizard were now eyeball to gelatinous eyeball, its jaw moving sideways on a dead fly. He shot upright again, feeling simultaneously unnerved and newly colossal.

A little further on, Alice pointed to a bird in flight, just the briefest agitation of its wings before it rested again on the warm thermal currents as if tethered by an invisible thread to the land.

'A kestrel, out looking for lunch.' She watched, enraptured. 'See how skilfully it controls its speed by flying into the wind. Isn't that the most beautiful thing you've ever seen?' She glanced in his direction, double-taking at what she saw. 'Oof. You're getting seriously burnt, you know. Here.' She knelt and tipped the last drops from the water bottle into the earth, scraping up the wetness and mixing it into a clay paste in the palm of her hand. 'Look. Like this.' She began to dab it on his face. A generous stripe across each cheekbone. Another down the length of his nose. The damp mud tightened on contact, creating a subtle contraction of the skin.

They were standing so close he could feel the exhalation of her warm breath against his cheek as she worked. 'Always fancied myself as a Native American.' He saw that she was frowning. 'Oops. Have I blundered again? What is it this time? Was that a "cultural appropriation" faux pas?'

She regarded him with a severe expression. 'Do I look like I'm laughing?' she said in a prim voice, before stepping back to survey him. 'Now me.' She extended the hand that held the clay paste towards him and, scooping some up, he made a few tentative dabs about her face. When he had finished, they stood surveying one another, an intent and wordless moment passing between them.

She let out a long exhalation. 'I've only just noticed. Our eyes are exactly the same colour. I mean like, *exactly*.'

He saw it was true. The silence lengthened. 'You were beginning to doubt, weren't you? I could see that.'

'I was.'

'I'm sorry, Alice. It's a lot to take in.'

He reached out to touch her arm but she only swallowed hard, before shrugging – *whatever*. 'This is definitely, without a shadow of doubt, the weirdest thing that has ever happened to me . . .' She looked down, her eyes welling, and though they resumed their journey, he sensed that Alice now walked in a daze. His long-lost daughter walking beside him. His long-lost daughter walking in perfect step. William began to whistle in a soft undertone, as an unexpected peace settled within. He watched the ease of the kestrel's gliding flight with a new attentiveness as they walked. So that's what those hovering creatures were up to. All those many times he had seen them from the car and never thought to wonder. Far beyond the kestrel, the pale disc of moon still hung, as if abandoned by the night.

Cressida was too distracted by the onset of a panic attack to note either the pale moon hanging so ethereally above the garden or the slow twisting wisps of cloud that intermittently obscured it. Earlier the phone had rung and some unrecognised number had flashed up on the screen. But when she answered, there had been only silence before the line went dead. *Where on earth were they? What could possibly have occurred to detain them this long?* She went to the window, but there was definitely no sign of William's jeep in the car park. She called his phone and left yet another waspish message when it went straight through to voicemail again. He must be showing off the charms of the island to Alice. Doubtless lunch in a delightful *chiringuito* on some unspoilt bay had by now rolled into a refreshing swim from one of his favourite hidden beaches somewhere. They would return at some point – father and daughter both glowing at their blossoming alliance. He had lost Jess but gained this newly minted doppelgänger. After a brief tussle with her conscience she went to the bathroom and took out the secret supply of pills she had stockpiled to get her through the weekend. *The One to Start With and the One to Stay With.* She gulped the tiny tablet down. Now that the press of workers had all retired for siesta, a blessed if temporary quiet had fallen on the house and gardens, a quiet that married with the blessed pharmaceutical calm that now steadily rose within.

Only Rene worked on despite the heat of the midday sun. Through the window she could see him bent low, pulling clumps of grass that had seeded themselves amongst the lavender bushes. They were a race blessed with extraordinary physical stamina, she thought musingly as she watched him. It was their enigmatically smiling demeanour, together with this wiry vigour, that made them so favoured as domestic workers. Their religious ardour could be a puzzle though. When Mary took the children to the beach she remained fully clothed, even when she took them into the sea. She said the priest had taught her that to be naked in any circumstances was a mortal sin. She seemed so chaste that Cressida sometimes wondered how Rene and Mary had ever contrived to conceive their daughter.

Rene had taken his shirt off and the sinewy musculature of his tanned back and forearms shifted in complex undulations as he worked. His years of manual labour had earned him the sculptured physique of a lean athlete. She looked at her watch. In less than an hour there would be a rush of returning workers. Followed at some point by Mary and the children. Together with the guests. But for now, the rows of sunloungers stretched away, blessedly vacant. She leant out of the window.

'Rene.' At first, he didn't hear her. She called again, and this time he looked up towards the house, screening his eyes against the dazzle of the sky. 'Could I borrow you for a moment? I need your help with something.'

She watched while he set down his secateurs and peeled off each glove, before pulling on his shirt and disappearing around the side of the house. She listened for his footsteps. But like Mary, he moved so habitually in silence that it wasn't until he reached the top of the stairs that she caught a faint movement and, hastening to slide the sleeve of her silk bathrobe from her shoulder, smoothed her hair back from her face. A second later he appeared in the doorway, where he remained, not quite meeting her eye.

'I'm so sorry to trouble you, Rene.'

'No problem, madam.'

'The thing is. Now that the house is so quiet, I hoped a quick swim might destress me. Would you be a darling and put some sun cream on my shoulders? I have a beautiful backless dress I'm determined to wear tonight and I'll never forgive myself if I burn.'

A look of profound discomfort fleeted across his face. He looked back the way he had come to the stairs. Then held his hands out, teetering at the threshold of the door as if an invisible barrier prevented him from progressing any further.

'I have been digging, madam.' He made as if to turn for the door again.

'Don't be silly. You were wearing gloves. I was watching you. And please don't call me "madam", Rene. You know how much I hate it . . .'

'I ask Mary if she . . .'

'Mary has taken the children to the beach. I'm not expecting them back for ages. There's no one at home but you and me . . .'

He came into the room moving in an awkward crab-like manner, with his eyes on the floor. She sat down on the edge of the bed, dropping the other sleeve, before handing him the bottle of sun lotion over one shoulder with a smile she hoped was irresistibly coquettish. She felt the mattress dip as he perched on the spot she had indicated and closed her eyes. She couldn't recall a time when they had ever been in such close proximity before. He smelt of salt and earth. For a fleeting moment it felt as if all the stars and planets were aligned, as if the world hung perfectly poised and ripe with possibility. She heard the apprehensive exhalation of his breath and the snap of the bottle being opened. Heard the squirt of cream and after a fractional pause felt the cool perfumed balm being applied in a patting, perfunctory fashion. Her eyes snapped open again. 'Gently, Rene, gently. My goodness! Anyone would think you were basting a chicken!'

Though his hand slowed, his touch remained workmanlike. Yet it sent shock waves through her. The longing for a human connection was hard-wired, she thought. In this moment of proximity, she could have wept for its long absence.

'Are you happy, Rene?'

'Happy?' The upward inflexion was guarded.

'You and Mary. Are you happy with your lives? Is everything OK?'

'Yes. Always happy, madam.'

His response was so determinedly lifeless, she was about to turn to him with a new lighthearted admonishment, when she saw with a jolt that the dressing-table mirror had caught their reflection deep in its shadows. It was hard to be sure but for a moment it looked exactly like he might be . . . No, there was no ambiguity about it at all. She could see only too clearly that he was grimacing.

'OK, Rene. That will do.' She spun about and snatched the bottle of sun cream from him, mortification like bleach swilling through her veins – but before she could say another word he had sprung to his feet and darted out through the door, raising his hand in a gesture of farewell that could just as readily have been an expression of heartfelt relief. Moments later she discovered, when she dared creep to the window again, that he had once more resumed his work, crouching over the lavender bushes as if there had never been any interruption to his labours. Though this time, he kept his shirt on, working with a certain stiffness of posture, as if conscious of the possibility of her eyes upon him. It was extraordinary how eloquent a turned back could be, she thought, tossing her head to affect an indifference she only wished she actually felt.

Having descended the steeply wooded hill, the path now emerged into farmland that opened up on every side. They appeared to have entered an Arcadian valley, the light that slanted through the leaves somehow softer and more reve-latory, their way bordered now by ancient stone walls. They passed a harvested field where cylindrical bales of hay were stacked high. Then a grove of almond and olive trees. It was the distant crowing of a cockerel that made them hasten their step. A little further a herd of sheep tinted red by the earth stopped their grazing to observe them with faces of blank senility, long strands of grass drooping from their slack mouths. Then moments later they rounded a corner and came upon a makeshift kennel set back from the path. At the sight of them, a pack of *podenco* hunting dogs surged against the wire mesh in a cacophony of barking. William and Alice walked on, following the trail until they arrived at a semi-derelict stone farmhouse hunkered low to the land with scattered outhouses half obscured by thickets of prickly pear. William surveyed the ancient house, with its cluster of cuboid rooms and flat roof, before clapping his hands.

'Well, hallelujah! Human beings. Civilisation. We are saved Alice . . .'

He looked about them. Whoever lived here was sitting on a veritable gold mine. A handsome old finca with all its original features intact. And surrounded by such an abundance of land. There were even distant views of the sea through the trees. 'And what a gem we have stumbled upon! They say this style of building dates back to Neolithic times . . .'

As they drew nearer still, the battered outhouses appeared to have been patched up over generations and from one of them arose the shrill keening of a pig. A handful of chickens burst up almost from under their feet, scattering away between the gnarled fruit trees with loud squawks of protest. William followed Alice across a makeshift yard, where sheets were drying on a line and an old wooden cart had been left so long exposed to the elements, it was half rotten.

The front door of the main house stood ajar, screened by beaded curtains, and in response to Alice's call, an elderly man emerged from its shadowed depths. Slight of frame, his puckish face observed them both with bright eyes. He appeared entirely unperturbed to find two strangers with mud-daubed faces on his doorstep. Summoned by his call, a white-haired woman appeared at his side, her plain workmanlike features and sturdy build making her considerably more imposing than her dapper husband.

'So sorry to trouble you but we're lost and need to borrow a phone.' William crooked his thumb and forefinger to his ear as Alice translated, conscious of how they both towered over the diminutive pair. The couple regarded them with expressions that were neither friendly nor hostile, before exchanging a few words and curtly beckoning them in.

They found themselves in a dimly lit living space with a high wooden-beamed ceiling and dirt floor. The room was filled with myriad objects both random and useful, giving an impression of simultaneous profusion and order as the sun slanted in through the dusty windows, falling in motefilled columns of light that revealed a timeless world, shelves stacked with old-fashioned knick-knacks and family photographs, together with a variety of musical instruments. Above their heads, the wooden beams were looped with the dusty ropes of cobwebs that must have gathered undisturbed for decades. Alice stood looking about her before letting out an appreciative sigh.

'It's exactly like a hobbit house that just sprouted out of the land one day.'

'And in a sense it did. The Ibicencos would build with whatever they had on hand. Rock for the walls, lime for whitewash, juniper to make the roof.' He passed a hand over the flaking plaster walls causing a little patter of lime dust to fall. 'And yet here it is, still standing solid as a rock five hundred years later.'

In the kitchen, buckets of goat's curd in varying stages of preparation had been set to one side. Here too there was the same simultaneous impression of spartan order countered by an abundance of produce. Old-fashioned kitchen implements hanging from nails, bowls fashioned from dry gourds heaped with eggs, handmade baskets overspilling with lemons. William saw that two little girls had come to peek at them with fascination, shyly hiding behind the door. The man pointed at one of the faded photographs on the shelf in which a smiling woman embraced the little girls. 'Britanic.'

Alice frowned. 'I think he's saying that the woman in the picture is British.' The man nodded his head with vigour. 'Si, vindrà.'

The old woman made a gesture of someone steering before pointing at the clock on the wall and then the floor.

'Hauria d'arribar en breu.' William looked at Alice for enlightenment.

'Something about the woman arriving at any moment. I've no idea what language they're speaking.'

'It's a kind of Catalan. The Ibicencos prefer not to use Spanish.'

The woman indicated that they should each take one of the wicker chairs, and though they did as she bid, the chairs were so small he felt even more like a clumsy interloper and an awkward silence fell upon the room. The small girls had by now slid into the room and along the wall like geckos, and though their palms remained pressed against the plasterwork as if poised to make a quick exit, both now stood inspecting the visitors, exchanging whispered observations from behind cupped hands. When Alice asked them in Spanish for their names, they only stared back at her with wide, unblinking eyes, until at length the silence was broken by a volley of barking from the caged hunting dogs and then, moments later, by the low rumble of a car coming down the drive. The old man raised a declarative finger. 'Veure! Agui esta!'

The car idled for a moment outside, followed by the clunk of a door closing and the sound of farewells, then the car backing up and receding away again down the track. After a moment, a darkhaired woman – at once recognisable from the photograph as the mother of the children – stepped into the kitchen and set down a basket filled with homemade loaves of bread. William leapt up, offering his most charming smile, and she stopped in surprise at the sight of them.

'Hi.' Alice got up to offer her hand, but the woman made no attempt to reciprocate, her arm remaining stiffly at her side, her waxen face regarding them with undisguised suspicion.

'What's all this, then?' She spoke in a broad Yorkshire accent.

'We were heading for the coastal path and somehow got ourselves completely lost. We were hoping you might be kind enough to lend us your phone.'

'Well me phone's got no credit left. And me husband's not here. So you're out of luck.'

She began unloading the loaves of bread onto the table, thumping them down, before peeling some euros from a small wad and begrudgingly tossing them in front of the old man.

'And me in-laws don't have any truck with newfangled things, so they're not going to be much use to you either.' She glanced with venom at the elderly couple, who listened with uncomprehending expressions. 'Haven't spoken to them for months anyway. They hate me and I hate them. Simple as that.'

Her tone was oddly matter-of-fact given the rancour of her words. The couple were called Vincent and Catalina, the woman explained, and her husband, Vincent junior, was a fisherman and the elderly couple's only child. She had been working in a local bar when she met him. Fancied himself as a bit of a Romeo in those days. For a moment she was lost in gloomy reverie. But she hadn't spoken a word of Spanish and he not a word of English. How barmy was that? 'And now look where I've ended up, daft cow that I am! Stuck miles from anywhere, with a couple of small children to worry about and not so much as two pennies to rub together.' She glanced with loathing at her inlaws.

'And it all looked so idyllic when we arrived.' Alice sounded crestfallen.

'Idyllic.' The woman emitted a bitter laugh. 'Like living in the bloody dark ages, more like.'

William cast a discreet glance at his watch. They'd just have to move on, find another house. He was about to clear his throat to explain that they would be on their way again, when the woman thrust a heavy bucket filled with food scraps into his arms, jerking her head to indicate he should follow. The two little girls brought up the rear.

'If you ever wanted to sell, you'd be amazed at the kind of prices an old finca like this can command these days,' he said as he followed her out. 'There was a time when people thought the north of the island too remote. Now everyone dreams of a secluded house with plenty of land. You wouldn't believe what people are prepared to pay for privacy and a sea view.'

The woman shook her head. 'Me husband sell? He were born in the house. His family have lived here for hundreds of years. Everyone round here's related. Cousins marry cousins. There are feuds that go back so many generations no one has the foggiest idea what they're actually about.'

As they crossed the sun-baked yard towards the warren of animal pens, William was only half listening, distracted by the handsome terraces that opened up about them, descending in a series of concentric crescents bordered by drystone walls and handsomely stocked with mature fruit trees. There were pomegranates ripening, and beyond them bright spots of oranges and lemons, so prolific the branches were bowed to the ground. At least one of the terraces offered a wide expanse easily big enough to site a pool. He walked about the weed-strewn courtyard, and wandered through the warren of half-fallen animal corrals and outhouses, ducking beneath the low doorways. One of the outhouses was filled with hay, another with mouldering tackle for a mule. Knock this warren of rooms through and you could easily create a series of charming bedroom suites. Put up a pergola along the south flank of the house to create a *plein air* dining area and outdoor kitchen. Restore this half-derelict outhouse to serve as the tech room. It wouldn't take much to turn it round. He defied any man of such patently modest means to resist once he saw the colour of William's money. He strolled about, ideas and plans whirring at lightning speed through his mind's eye.

The woman had stopped at the open door of one of the outhouses. Peering into the gloom, he saw an obese pig lying on its side. She took the bucket from him, upending it into the pen as the pig struggled to its feet, emitting snorts of pleasure.

'Out here a daughter-in-law's just a skivvy,' she went on in an aggrieved tone. 'Someone to cook and clean and mind the farm while the in-laws put their feet up. Only – I'm not bloody having it anymore, am I?' She addressed the question to the little girls, who looked back with impassive expressions, as if they'd heard it many times before. 'I'm not.' She looked at

William with a defiant glare. 'Soon as I've scraped together enough money, I'll take my girls and go back to Yorkshire. Won't see us for dust.'

Returning to the house, they found Catalina showing Alice an album of black-and-white photographs of her family dressed in traditional peasant clothes, formally seated in an old-fashioned portrait studio. He heard the thin puttering of a scooter coming down the track, followed by a renewed cacophony from the kennelled dogs.

'Well, well, well – looks like you might be in luck on the phone front after all. Here's his lordship returning to grace us with his presence.'

She went to the sink and busied herself clattering pans in defiant readiness, and moments later a short man with a swarthy handsome face entered the room holding a bucket whose contents he tipped into the sink, a flash of silver fish sliding in a brief cascade. William sprang to his feet in readiness as the older of the two girls said something to her father – and Vincent appeared to be reaching for the phone that protruded from his breast pocket as he turned to glance at the visitors. But his expression inexplicably darkened as he took William in, and instead of proffering the phone, he wheeled about to address his wife in an indignant tone.

'He says he knows you,' she said.

William shook his head in confusion. 'I beg your pardon?'

'Was you on the mountain road heading towards Sant Joan yesterday afternoon?'

He nodded. 'I was . . .'

'He were on his way to deliver a hundred lobster to a private party, when the car broke down. Says he tried to flag you down but you only drove straight past. Says you've got a right bloody cheek coming here, asking him for a favour after leaving him so high and dry.'

William examined the man more closely as Vincent junior glowered at him, noting the perspiration that beaded the man's upper lip. A dim recollection of an Ibicenco standing beside a broken-down car at the top of that hill en route to the Cala Conta site came to him.

Vincent junior angrily interjected again, this time addressing his elderly parents, and his mother tsked with disapproval at whatever it was her son was telling her, before turning to regard William with a vexed shake of her head.

'He's saying he were up from dawn to dusk catching lobster,' the woman said. 'Then the whole lot went bad in the sun while he waited for a lift and so we won't see a penny for all his trouble. And we were relying on that money.' The woman's guppy mouth heralded tears. 'So much for my escape fund . . .'

William recalled Cressida's plans to serve lobster and scratched the nape of his neck, grimacing. This situation was getting more tricky by the moment. The fisherman stepped towards him, his guttural tirade coming again like rat-tat-tat gunfire, one finger stabbing the air only inches from William's chest.

'What's he saying now?' William asked, turning to the woman in alarm.

'He's cursing you and all your ancestors . . .'

The woman spoke sharply to her husband in Ibicenco. Whatever it was she said seemed to have the desired effect because he reached to adjust his genitals as if to temper his fury, before backing away with an angry snort. At the door he picked up the empty bucket before bringing it down with such a crash that it clattered sideways across the floor, at which both girls ran with a shriek from the room. Then with a final oath, he strode after his daughters and from outside in the courtyard came a panicked squawking as if the chickens were trying to evade an angry kick.

It occurred to William that the man might well be going to get his gun. All those hunting dogs housed in the kennels meant he must certainly have firearms somewhere. They hastened through the fly curtain and out into the blinding sunlight of the courtyard again. William cast one last covetous eye over the farm, wondering how he could ever find it again. The place might be remote, but with one of those turbo-charged boosters, it shouldn't be too difficult to get a decent Wi-Fi connection up here. The dirt track to the house would have to be tarmacked. Permission to connect to the mains secured and pylons erected. He would return with a peace offering to begin negotiations once tempers had cooled. The woman was explaining to Alice how to find the coastal path as he reached into his pocket for a business card. But finding only the roll of banknotes he'd seized that morning, he thrust the money into the woman's palm instead. 'Here. For your escape fund. The least I can do.'

The woman assessed the roll of money and then William, before whisking the wad out of sight, her eyes darting all the while over their shoulder. 'Best to get off sharpish.' She tapped a finger to her temple. 'No telling what he might do.'

By the time Cressida had completed her swim, she found the house filled with the noise of work resuming. The rumble of trolleys being dragged to and fro along the gravel paths was accompanied by a booming soundcheck that came and went and the roar of yet more delivery trucks trundling down the long driveway.

She bent towards the magnifying mirror on her dressing-table to examine the enlarged planes of her face, as she began applying her makeup for the party. It was like looking at the surface of the moon. So many shameful yet fascinating indentations and flaws. A giant nostril rearing into sight, filling the frame of the mirror like a cavern deep enough to swallow her whole. Unnerved, she stepped back to inspect herself as the world would see her, widening her eyes and pouting.

'Mummy's doing her mirror face,' Lola would have cried with mocking glee if she were on hand to observe her.

But there would come a time when Lola too would understand the treacherous business of mirrors. Cressida had learnt to her cost that it was never wise to come upon one unawares. Morale might plummet if a tolerable countenance wasn't prepared in readiness. She could never quite reconcile herself to the face that revealed itself when she unexpectedly caught sight of it in repose. Yet even with her face held in careful readiness, the effect was unreliable. Between one mirror and the next the impression of a relatively youthful countenance could, depending on the arrangement of light, be superseded within minutes by a tired and ageing one. She had no idea which version most resembled any objective reality. Increasingly these days, the cruel reflective square of silver unflinchingly charted how gravity weighted her mouth and jawline, and corded her neck, as little by little the face of her autumn years crept upon her.

She sat for some while, deep in thought. The discovery of Alice's existence appeared such a manifestly touching event from the outside. When the news of William's long-lost daughter broke upon them, after her initial shock, it felt too churlish to share her worries with William about the practical ramifications. For in one fell swoop not only had Lola been displaced as the eldest child and only daughter but it could surely be no more than a matter of time before William was trying to persuade Cressida that his estate would now have to be split three ways instead of two. Her humph of indignation misted the mirror. Well, if so – she could just make out her newly made-up eyes blinking through the condensation – he was about to discover a considerably less compliant side to her.

She thought of all those years he had been so adamant he didn't want children. At first it hadn't worried her at all. Quite the contrary. She had always been so ambivalent about the prospect of parenthood herself that she was relieved to find themselves so in alignment on the issue. But as the years passed and many of their circle started to produce offspring, much to her surprise an elemental maternal yearning began to take root in her. Yet William had remained intractable on the subject, and soon subtle and then not so subtle tensions began to open up between them. Tensions that crystallised over time into a complete stand-off. Eventually, the stand-off was resolved after a surprise contraceptive mishap and, with a year to go to her fortieth birthday, Lola had been the fortuitous outcome. Two years later, and another contraceptive mishap meant that Joe had completed the family. After which, William, accusing her of duping him twice over, had refused any further physical intimacy, their stand-off over children replaced by a new stand-off over sex.

One early morning not so long ago, she had swum out to a favourite cave in a nearby bay, where she was startled to disturb a couple making love in the shadowed depths of the seaweed-scented cavern. They had both appeared high as kites, uncoupling without a trace of self-consciousness at her arrival, eager to share stories of their 'totally crazy night'. Once home she was peeling off her wet costume when William happened to step into the bedroom, and she had flown at him, pressing her lips to his. At which he had stepped away, wiping his mouth with the back of his hand.

'Woah. Steady on there, old girl!' he had said, taking up his phone with a tight little laugh and soon losing himself in it.

A thought was waiting to be thought and it coagulated for the first time with a painful clarity. Wasn't his steadfast resistance to having children for all those years only further evidence that he must have known all along he already had one?

She made her way down the corridor to William's study and walked about, examining his things, poking the architect's model of Cala Conta into line with her foot. Then she lifted out the bottle of whisky from behind the books and, seeing it was almost empty, replaced it with an irritated click of the tongue. She went back to the bedroom, glancing down over the west side where scores of workers were making their final preparations.

In the bathroom she picked up her electric toothbrush. It was a new state-of-the-art number whose vibrating vigour made her think of an angry bumblebee. *Designed to effectively lift and power away plaque, leaving behind nothing but an astonishing clean.* More recently, however, she had been pleasantly surprised to discover an astonishing additional purpose for it. One the manufacturers had neglected to detail in their instruction manual. *Marriage unravelling? Who needs a love life when you have this engineered to perform, oscillating, rotating, pulsating technological breakthrough instead!* Switching it to its lowest speed, she placed the flat back of the buzzing brush between her legs and within moments had fallen, moaning, first to her knees and then very soon, poleaxed, to the floor.

Follow the path up and over the next hill, the woman had told them, and once they descended the far side, they would eventually arrive at the sea. There the path would fork, the left branch hugging the coast to take Alice south, while the other would bring William to an asphalt road where he might, with luck, be able to hitch a lift home. Alice walked ahead, keeping up the pace despite the improbably steep incline. The sooner they got to the coastal path, the sooner they would be free of one another. The thought lent renewed energy to her step.

'Well, that was a bit alarming!' Struggling for breath, William had managed to catch up with her, but she neither turned nor slowed her pace. No point in saying anything. The man was a lost cause.

'I promise you, Alice. I barely saw him. It all happened in the blink of an eye.'

She rolled her eyes. 'You made a choice. And the choice was to prioritise yourself.'

'Oh, and I suppose you would stop for a complete stranger in the middle of nowhere on a sweleteringly hot day?' He swiped away the rivulets of sweat that ran down his face and stung his eyes.

'I think the question is more – why would you *not* stop for a complete stranger on a hot day in the middle of nowhere! Of course I would . . .'

'Then once again I must concede the moral high ground to you. I see it is your role to inhabit the dizzying peaks of saintliness, while I dwell forever in the valley of the sinner.'

At the top of the hill, the sea finally stretched out before them in a wide expanse of blue. Alice raised her arms in silent celebration, looking heavenwards as if to thank the powers that be.

'Looks like we will both shortly be free to go our separate ways again and resume our respective lives of saint and sinner without impediment,' he said in a stiff voice.

'Yup.' Alice was fishing around in her backpack before bringing out a pouch of tobacco and papers. 'Hallelujah and praise the Lord for small mercies, hey . . .' She began to construct a cigarette as they walked.

He observed her in surprise. 'I didn't know you smoked . . .'

'Well, let's be honest. The list of what you don't know about me remains pretty extensive.' Having fashioned the cigarette, she fished around in the bottom of her bag again for a lighter. She lit the cigarette before taking in a long inhalation and emitting a neat series of smoke rings at the sky. 'I can give you

a quick heads-up before we part if you like. Just the headlines.'
She glanced over to check she had his full attention. 'I've
been in an on/off relationship with someone called Franny.
Though right now we're more off than on. She thinks I have
commitment issues. And she's a therapist, so annoyingly she
tends to know what she's talking about. We have a dog called
Whizzer, who's our delinquent surrogate child. And what else?
Oh, and I'm currently in a spot of trouble with the law.'

He nodded. 'Yes – well, that much I do know.' She glanced
at him in surprise.

'Cressida found the court summons in your room after you
left. What did you do?'

She blew out another long exhalation of smoke. 'Hijacked
a train.'

Now it was his turn to blink in surprise.

'I was dressed as a canary at the time.'

He shook his head, as if trying to dislodge whatever was
impeding the sentence from making sense, before bursting
into laughter.

'Nice. The canary in the mine. Of course you were!' Despite
herself, she found she was laughing too. 'That's priceless . . .'
He clapped his hands.

'We were targeting a coal-fired power station.'

'And the train was taking coal to the power station?'

'Exactly. In North Yorkshire. It wasn't remotely funny at the
time though. I was absolutely terrified. We flagged the train
down, then manacled ourselves to one of the wheels. It took

them sixteen hours to find the right specialist equipment to cut us free. But our intention was always to get arrested. And . . .' She shrugged. 'We were.'

'Why on earth would you want to be arrested?'

'Go to court and you're guaranteed good media coverage. Though of course it's different for someone like me. When you're black the whole judicial process is weighted against you right from the get-go. And a criminal record is far more likely to mess up your career prospects. So – you know – it's certainly not something I undertook lightly.'

'Alice. Sweetheart.' He looked over his sunglasses at her. 'Black? I don't think so. Mixed race might be nearer the mark.' A starburst of outrage momentarily blinded her.

'Oh, you think so, do you? I had no idea you were an expert on ethnicity.'

'OK. Put it this way. By my count, three of your four grandparents were white.'

'Trust me. When I walk down the street, when I go to a job interview, people see a black woman, OK.'

'Christ.' He rubbed his eyes behind his sunglasses as if to remove the dust of confusion. 'You Gen-Zers are so *invested* in all this stuff.'

'Hard to see how investing in diversity, equity and inclusion could be controversial.'

'OK, OK. RIP the white male and all that. I'm toast. I get it. I submit. Fair dos.'

She observed the grey that flecked his hair, the faint creases at the edge of each eye, and exhaled a long slow breath before forcing a smile.

'Look. I would happily debate identity politics with you. But given that it's not long till we go our separate ways, let's just try to avoid the obvious minefields, shall we?'

'Black it is, then.' He was nodding emphatically. 'Point taken.' He walked in silence, appearing to turn it all over. 'And how do you feel about the possibility of spending time in jail?'

She considered his question for a moment, feeling the familiar heaviness weight her heart. 'When I read how our very future hangs by a thread, I honestly don't feel I have much choice. It seems a small sacrifice in the grand scheme of things.'

He reached out to touch her arm. 'I do get it. You know that, don't you?'

'You so don't.'

'I'm sure that somehow or other, your generation can find a way to figure it all out.'

She turned on him with fury.

'Right. So that's you off the hook, then. Your generation got us into this mess but it's down to mine to sort it out. Just as long as you don't personally have to make any compromises to the way you live, right? I mean – God forbid you should have to do that.'

'Alice. Honestly. Do you really think that if I ripped out my lawn – allowed my swimming pools to run dry – if I never took another plane ride – that it would make one jot of difference?'

'I genuinely don't understand.'

'What?'

'Your wilful blindness. We only have one home. Here it is.' She gestured urgently to indicate the trees, the mountains, the great sweep of sea. 'Our only hope now is for us each to become its fiercest custodian.'

He looked pensive, something intensely sad in his expression. She thought perhaps her words had struck home. Instead. 'You just don't give up, do you? I swear to God, you are your mother reincarnated. It's truly uncanny . . .'

Your mother. The noun hung on the air between them. They were like cautious skaters crossing thin ice together, she thought. So much left unsaid. The well-honed arguments of activism withered on her lips. She felt unutterably weary. And if she was honest, she envied him. She wanted nothing more than to slip the noose of knowing. She would give anything to be able to close her mind to the darker uncertainties.

'She would have been so incredibly proud of you. I hope you know that.'

She tried to put it away but the question rose irrepressibly to her lips. 'So, was it a love thing, or just a one-night stand?'

His bark of laughter was more an expression of being caught off guard than mirth. 'Was it a love thing? Christ. What a wonderfully old-fashioned question, Alice!'

'Well?'

Alice waited with impatience as he struggled to summon an answer.

'Well . . . Your mother and I met in our first year of college. And I can't deny that I was pretty instantly smitten. Everyone was. She was one of those people who burn very brightly. You know, once encountered, never forgotten.'

He flashed an absent smile in her direction.

'But the thing was – you had to tread with care – because anyone who knew her would tell you that Jess was a piece of work. Ate men for breakfast. Was famous for it. So, a wise man kept his distance.'

'Right. So you were in love.'

A subterranean spasm fleeted across his features.

'Yes, OK. I was crazy about her. Though sadly it was unrequited.' His smile was rueful.

As they turned the corner, she saw that they had finally arrived at the place where the path divided, one track following the coast, the other, marked by a walkers' sign, striking left up the hill, just as the woman had described. She stopped.

'So. Guess this is where we say our goodbyes, then.'

He looked at his watch. 'A little later than I expected. But. We seem to have emerged in one piece. Still just about on speaking terms at any rate. Are you absolutely sure this is what you want to do?'

'I'm absolutely certain.' She was nodding emphatically. 'So long then, William.' She extended her hand.

But rolling his eyes at her formality, he stepped forward to offer her an embrace instead. Only somehow, in the awkward dance of confusion, his shoe slid on a scree of rocks and he fell sideways, landing with a sickening thump at her feet.

'Christ.' He had curled into a foetal ball of pain and it was a while before he was able to do anything but groan and writhe. At length he managed to slide the injured leg forward to reveal an ankle already swelling and discoloured. 'Fuck, fuck, fuck.'

She crouched down to examine it. 'OK. Don't worry. Nothing broken. Just needs some compression.' She spoke with the cool authority bestowed on her by her activist training and gesturing with impatience at him to remove his shirt, she tore it into strips before binding the ankle and raising his foot onto her backpack.

'And now you just sit tight . . .' She rose. 'While I go ahead and get help.'

The beach was packed with sunbathers whose semi-naked physiques exhibited every possible variation of age and fitness. Dressed in old leggings and a baggy T-shirt, Mary sat under the shade of a sun parasol keeping one eye on Joe, who was dabbling his feet at the water's edge, while she plaited Lola's hair.

When the *banyaga* talked about 'homesickness', it was an apt term. For days now she had felt nauseous with longing. More than anything, she yearned to see her daughter again. But she also missed being amongst people who resembled her, ate like her and spoke her language. It was two years since Mary last returned to her village, a trip which had passed in a cheerful round of visits and expeditions – and on Sunday she and Rene had gone to church with Angel and her mother. After the service, members of the congregation had clustered about them, eager to hear their news. Everyone had family members scattered across the world and were hungry for updates on life overseas. Mary had been proud to tell them about the life they had made for themselves in Ibiza and to see for herself the benefits their financial support was bestowing on so many.

She had been raised to serve her church, family and community. And it was this sense of being in service that gave her the determination to endure, to strive, to prosper – an ethos so ubiquitous in her culture, she had never thought to question it until she arrived in Europe.

Once, early in her employment, she had been startled to overhear Cressida talking in a distressed tone Mary had never heard before. When she paused to peek through a gap in the half-open door, she saw that Cressida was conversing with someone on her iPad.

'I don't know who I am anymore,' Cressida was saying in a tear-choked voice. 'I wake up in the morning – and I think – I think – *what is the point of me?*' And though Mary couldn't quite catch whatever it was the unseen listener said in response, she remembered still the terrible primal despair of Cressida's weeping.

Afterwards Mary had wondered about madam's distress and who this person might be who received her secrets like a priest. It was disorientating to hear her sounding so lost as she sat amidst the manifest abundance of her life.

Mary secured Lola's plait with a hairband and folded her arms about her, touching her lips to Lola's crown. Her childish scent held a kinetic charge so deeply hard-wired into Mary's maternal circuitry that it always unsettled and comforted her in equal measure. She thought about her last Skype call with Angel.

'Please will you and Tatay come to my confirmation, Nanay? Please?' her daughter had implored, leaning forward into the camera so that only her eyes filled the frame. 'Pleeease . . .'

'I will try my best, OK,' Mary had assured her, reaching out to touch the screen. A sober resolve settled upon her at the recollection of that promise.

Dear Lord, please help us in our hour of need. She crooked her head skywards, waiting for a sign. But if the Lord was listening, he made no move to show it. And realising the moment had arrived, that she could wait no longer, she crossed herself to ward off bad spirits, collecting their things up in haste before her resolve should diminish. A man selling sliced watermelon held out his basket of wares to her but she waved him away. She called out to Joe and Lola. 'We go home now, OK. See Mummy before party. Hope Mummy in good mood.'

Why was it always that you'd no sooner shot up a ladder than you were slipping down a snake? William sat amongst the shriek of cicadas, gazing at the sea, with his foot propped up on the bag. At least the pain had receded to a dull throb. Hazy yachts were adrift on a body of hazy water that rose to merge with hazy sky. He had left first thing this morning with the expectation he would be back within the hour. Now here he was in the – he checked his watch again – in the late afternoon, not only still hopelessly lost but now hopelessly incapacitated too. He thought of Cressida. She would be in her element, marshalling the troops. Doubtless still fuming and with any luck relieved not to have him underfoot. But at least he now had a bona fide injury to explain his late return. He roused himself with a sigh, flipping over his discarded sandals to examine their frictionless soles. *Handcrafted in Italy by artisans – guaranteed to lend comfort and style to every outfit.* The sole had come completely adrift from its base. No wonder he had slipped. The bloody things might lend comfort and style to every outfit but they obviously weren't intended to be actually walked in. He lobbed first one and then the other into the sea, where they landed with a satisfying splash.

He looked about him, noticing how a golden haze was stealing over everything as the sun began its long afternoon descent to the west. The rising vegetal perfume of the land rose up to fill his nostrils. Overhead the violet-tinged sky was filled with noisy swifts, who dropped on the air currents before ascending and falling again, hundreds of them criss-crossing in every direction. *Could that be anything other than an expression of joy,* he wondered? *A recreational surfing of the heavens.* The very air about him oscillated with their piercingly melodic squeaks and he felt all at once more keenly alive than he had done in years.

In his early life, he had experienced the pleasant sensation of being carried by unseen currents that moved always in his favour, taking him on from university quite naturally into banking, from where his steadily building success and influence had led to a welcome glow of public affirmation and growing material comfort. New possibilities had opened up in a series of ever expanding ripples. At Goldman Sachs he was soon subsumed by a culture in which high-minded principles were at best an irrelevance and at worst an active impediment. But he had always prided himself on his chameleon-like tendencies. He would run with the pack until the time came when he might take stock. Stand for something. Evolve an ethos. Yet somehow . . . Somehow that time had never quite arrived.

When he met Jess at college, her political engagement had dazzled him. He had never met anyone like her before. To find himself within earshot of her at a table in mid-discourse on the state of the world was invigorating. She galvanised him into marshalling his thoughts and, more than once, to go away and furnish himself with enough facts to assemble an intelligent counter-argument of his own. For he soon discovered that taking an opposing view was a surefire way to engage her, and it roused him to see her eyes flash as her voice rose in exasperation – even though he might be representing a position that in all honesty he felt no particular allegiance to. To draw her fire in debate, to successfully parry ideas with her, was to be momentarily elevated. After a particularly fierce exchange on the rights and wrongs of Israel and Zionism, the memory of their verbal swordplay had burnt in him for days afterwards.

What a funny old business it all was. He couldn't deny he'd always kept his foot on the accelerator, not only literally but metaphorically too. That he had been so intent on retaining his position in the fast lane, he had never wondered where he was actually heading, or considered any hidden costs he might be accruing as he flew. And now here was Alice, just like her mother, calling him to account. She would probably have something to say about the boat. He shook his head, wincing.

A sleek Ocean Alexander 65 he had fallen for in a state of elation after pulling off a particularly lucrative deal. A little beauty that, as its novelty value wore thin, had soon been spurned by his family for more landbased activities. As a result it now sat largely unused in the marina at Santa Eularia, where it nonetheless continued to run up bills with such rapidity it had come to feel more as if the boat owned him.

His sandals were still bobbing at the water's edge and it occurred to him that he should retrieve them before Alice returned. But as he inched his way forward to hook them out again, a subterranean movement caught his eye. Peering down into the briny depths, he glimpsed a dainty prehistoric creature sashaying along the ocean bed. It was moving as if on tiptoes, its powerful pincers raised at the ready. The only lobsters he had seen before had been lying deceased and resplendent on a mound of crushed ice, with an eye-watering price tag attached. So it was a shock to see how precise and balletic its movements were, despite its ceramic-like eyes, which shone with a beady chill.

'Guess you've come to avenge your squandered *compadres*,' he said out loud. 'And frankly, who can blame you.' But he'd no sooner leant forward to get a better look than the creature had shot backwards and vanished beneath the rocky overhang again. He plucked up a nearby stick before manoeuvring with difficulty onto his belly and probing the lobster's hiding place. At first only a billow of tiny pebbles emerged in a sideways drift. But then in a flash of goose-stepping legs and snapping pincers, the lobster darted out again, moving this time in a truculent war dance to see him off.

He would bag it and take it home as a gift for Cressida, he thought with a thrilled rush. Offer it humorously, in lieu of the spoilt delivery, and maybe get her to cut him a little slack by making her laugh. But every time he jabbed at it, the stick only slid through its pincers. He jabbed, the lobster snapped and he jabbed again, like an emboldened matador – and then the stick abruptly jolted in his hand as the goaded lobster finally seized it with such force that in his panic William yanked it up and out of the water, startled to find it now hanging only inches from his face. An armour-plated tail writhing to and fro. A horrible rattling sound. Bubbles frothing and clustering at its gills. Viewed at such extreme proximity, its alien-like form struck a terror so primitive in him it could only emanate from some ancestral memory deep in the amygdala and, with another involuntary convulsion, he dropped the stick, together with its alarming cargo, allowing both to fall with a crash back into the sea. He reared back, prompting his dislodged sunglasses to tumble too, before vanishing without trace into the briny depths.

He sat for some moments, gulping air and trying to compose himself. Over the thump of his heart he could hear the thin high timpani of distant whistling. He lay down. Perhaps auditory hallucinations were the first sign of sunstroke. Certainly, his face felt as if it was on fire. But the sound really did appear to be growing louder. He opened his eyes again. A small procession was coming towards him along the coastal path down which Alice had vanished. Dogs wheeled about the heels of four adults who carried between them a long, wide plank of wood. At their helm trotted three naked children. One of the children was playing a flute, while the other two beat time with sticks. William observed them as they drew nearer.

'Can you believe this?' Alice was smiling as they came abreast of him. 'I found these lovely people on a beach just over the hill. They're busy preparing for a solstice celebration but they've kindly agreed to help us.'

They laid the plinth down beside him, each taking one of his limbs apiece before lifting him onto it with great care. Then with an alarming lurching motion they swung the timber beam onto their shoulders, before turning back in the direction they'd just come. William laid back, attempting to resign himself to the loss of agency.

'And. You'll be glad to hear, I have a plan,' Alice said.

'Go on, then. I'm all ears. What on earth has the woman who stops trains dressed as a canary managed to dream up now?'

'This one involves a boat.'

'A boat?'

'Not your kind of boat. Nothing fancy. Just a plastic two-person kayak number.'

'You're right. A plastic kayak is most definitely not my kind of boat.'

One of the pall-bearers laughed. 'Listen, my friend. A kayak might not be your usual mode of transport, but it will get you to the marina in a jiffy. There'll be cabs to get you to your party. And a ferry bus to get your daughter to the port.'

William held on for dear life as the platform lurched sideways beneath him. 'OK, OK. This is now going from the sublime to the ridiculous . . . Let me be perfectly clear about this. I have absolutely no intention of trying to get anywhere in a kayak.'

'Ah. So, you're back. Good. Run and help the caterers find somewhere to stack their boxes, would you. They're in a bit of a tizzy.' Cressida was standing in front of the full-length mirror, frowning as she moved this way and that in her new party dress. She examined Mary for a moment, trying to discern from her demeanour if Rene had said anything to her. There was definitely something unusually agitated about her, almost as if she might be readying herself to make a speech of some kind. What a funny plain little thing she was, standing there with her hair scraped back in a ponytail and her feet jammed into those plastic flip-flops over the ankle socks she always wore, even as the temperatures soared. The impending evening was rushing towards them and Cressida gave only the scantiest of attention to Mary's request as she stepped with care into her new and improbably high heels. *A must-have! Wow your friends in the A-listers' red carpet favourite.* She hadn't worn high heels for years. Why had it ever seemed a good idea?

'A loan. For two thousand euros! My goodness . . .'

She turned back to the mirror, wondering again if the dress was really as becoming as she had first thought when she bought it, and it took a moment for her to resurface and discover that Mary still lingered at the door. How bloodless and strange she looked. Not like her usual self at all.

'I not understand. So is it yes or no, madam?'

'At any other time, we'd have loved to help. Of course we would. But I'm afraid this party has all but bankrupted us! When we win the lottery, I promise you'll be first in line. I'm so sorry . . .'

Cressida smoothed the dress over her hips, relieved to see her maid nod her head with an odd jerky motion, before hastening from the room without another word.

His four bearers carried William along the belly of a dried-out creek with steep flanks banked high on either side, passing through flowering oleander and grasses, before emerging between two boulders onto a small sandy bay. The sun was so blinding it took a moment for William's eyes to adjust. It was like stepping into the white-out of a flashbulb. He felt all at once dizzy and nauseous. There were whoops and whistles and he saw that the beach was clustered with naked figures who had stopped their preparations to clap his arrival. As they turned back to resume their tasks, the scene was strikingly timeless. A young woman was bending to tend an open fire, and a man was hanging wet clothes from a rope strung between two juniper trees, while nearby a group sat crosslegged in a circle, preparing food together. Nearby, a man with flowing white hair strummed a guitar, while a pixie-faced woman sang a soft accompaniment. Their very nakedness, together with the frugality of their belongings, was reminiscent of Stone Age settlers and he felt at once the discordance. Arriving like a maharaja on a bier, even in nothing but his shorts, he felt overdressed, the glint of the investment watch at his wrist a regrettable vulgarity. Most had face piercings or dreadlocked hair and the few that wore clothes were dressed in bandanas and loose harem pants, eclectic combinations that spoke of dusty travels through remote regions of Morocco and India. They were a familiar sight, part of the island's extensive subculture, many of whom manned the stalls at the hippy markets or gathered at the under-the-radar music events and sweat lodges. This was a community who had always intrigued him for their facility to live and thrive on a shoestring. As he was carried aloft through the crowds he caught a multitude of accented English, and snatches of Dutch, Italian, German and something that might even have been Estonian. A topless woman bedecked with silver jewellery approached, bringing water. Behind her a naked man bearing food. Alice introduced the woman. This was the person who'd given her a lift from the airport. Her name was Paloma. And now she was offering them her boat.

'For pity's sake, Alice. Someone here must have a phone.' He turned to appeal to the woman. 'Paloma. Surely the sensible thing would be to just call a cab.'

Paloma shook her head. 'We are far from anywhere and the track to get here is very bad. No cab would be willing to make that journey. I'm sorry.'

The pall-bearers set him down with care on the mounds of seagrass that lined the foreshore. On a large flat boulder a few feet away, William saw that people had made a collection of objects into a makeshift shrine. A handful of crystals. A seagull's feather. A cluster of fraying friendship bracelets. Someone was burning palo santo, and the pungent ecclesiastical smell stirred some residual memory of ritual in him. Something deeply known and long lost. Alice took out the contents of her pocket and laid them on the altar with care. A snail's shell, an acorn and a small pine cone. She made a namaste with her hands and bent her head.

It seemed an apt moment to try and appease the gods. After a moment's tussle, he came to a decision and, unclipping his watch, leant over to lay it reverently amongst the objects. An Audemars Piguet Royal Oak, with its steel case and octagonal bezel. *A timepiece that has borne witness to the greatest moments in history on the wrist of visionaries, virtuosos and pioneers.* When he came upon it during a business trip to Milan its understated elegance had been a *coup de foudre*. He rubbed his newly denuded wrist, noting the strip of white skin its removal had revealed. His worldly goods had branded him.

And now he had no worldly goods left except . . . He examined his left hand before taking off his wedding ring and laying it down beside the watch. *95% platinum. A symbol of shared happiness.* The pale strip of skin around his ring finger struck him as entirely apt. Sixteen years of marriage, now marked by nothing more than a ghostly absence.

They gulped down the food and drink, observing the sky's luminescence dim as the sun began its long descent towards the horizon. The idea of taking a boat was patently barmy. But it was also true that once they reached the marina, the cab ride home would take no time at all. That it would just be a matter of a lightning-quick shower, a clean linen shirt, a generous snifter of whisky – and he'd be ready to hit that party running. Already he was shaping the events of the day into an amusing party piece for his return.

Where have I been? he would say in an airy tone to his enthralled guests as he hobbled through the door. *I've been at a shamanic gathering on a remote beach, making offerings to the universe. So how did I get myself home? Well, my intrepid daughter nobly arranged to row her crippled father down the coast in a kayak.* How differently things appeared without a gnawing hunger and raging thirst to contend with.

'OK. Let's do it.'

The kayak awaited them at the water's edge and the bejewelled woman held its bowline steady as first William and then Alice climbed in. It took a little while to synchronise their strokes but once they hit their rhythm they were rewarded with a gratifying sensation of momentum, as the boat slid readily through the water.

'We've got this!' Alice cried out in triumph, bending to her oar.

'May the pure light within you guide your way,' Paloma called after them, touching her fingertips to the small gold head of the goddess Tanit that hung about her neck. A few well-wishers had joined her to wave them off. But very soon their well-wishers were no more than tiny specks on the coastline.

The field was big enough, but only just. The catering trucks, the dancers' Winnebago, the row of luxury portaloos now filled its modest proportions like a pop-up township. Impossible to recall how this had ever seemed a good idea. An assortment of waiters dressed in Moroccan tunics were being led by Rene towards the house as he rapidly briefed them over one shoulder. Two waitresses in diaphanous belly dancer's costumes were leaning against the trunk of a carob tree enjoying a quick cigarette, one of them recounting a story with much theatrical waving of hands while the other made up her face in a small mirror, exclaiming as she listened. Cressida stopped to beg for a cigarette, waiting while the girl fished through her handbag, passing first a cigarette and then a lighter. But though Cressida made several attempts to light it, her hands trembled too much to produce a flame, until eventually the girl took pity on her and reached over with a sympathetic click of her tongue to ignite it for her. Cressida walked away, taking quick tokes on the burning stem. But she'd never been much of a smoker and, after a few puffs, she stubbed it out and put it away in her clutch bag, wondering miserably if it might still be possible to cancel the whole event even at this late hour. How could she possibly go ahead without William? It was absurd. Better surely to send out a message on social media before leaving a cancellation notice tied to the gates. But the image of King Canute came to her, his hand raised to stop the incoming sea – and she regretfully relinquished the idea. She stopped to open her clutch bag again and take out the blister pack that held the last remaining pill, gulping it down.

A new image came to her, this time of William lying dead in a ditch somewhere, with the overturned car beside him. This was at once superseded by another image of William miraculously restored and striding across the field towards her. And it was true! Even now, there was still time for him to arrive and take his place beside her. But if he didn't – what on earth was she going to tell everyone? The smell of cooking onions from the tagine tent rose pungently on the air. She would just have to decide on a line and then stick to it. William has been unavoidably detained. A professional crisis of a confidential nature. And if midnight came and there was still no sign of him? Then she would have to call the police.

Not that she could imagine them being much help. These were island police, after all. She thought with despondency of the languor of Little and Large.

The camel was resisting all attempts to be led down the ramp from its transportation truck. Its handler was yanking hard on the harness while issuing a litany of what Cressida took to be Arabic profanities, as the poor creature's long bony-kneed legs buckled and slid against the struts of the metal ramp. Nearby, a boa constrictor lay coiled in its basket. All this ridiculous trouble and expense with no birthday recipient to manifest either surprise or joy. At last, cajoled onto solid ground, the camel emitted a low, mutinous grumble, before raising its stumpy tail and copiously spattering the earth with straw-flecked dung.

Alice and William rowed in slow unison as the sea transformed all about them into a vast sheet of shifting silver, the colour of the shoreline sliding into ever deepening shades of indigo and violet. In the far distance, a paddle boarder, bent to their oar, as if time was pleating back on itself, only for the tranquillity to be disrupted by the contemporary throb of an engine as a motorboat towing a waterskier swept into sight. She watched the boat and skier round the thickly wooded promontory before vanishing into the next bay as the sky grew ever dimmer.

'Look at us! We've gone completely crackers. Stark raving mad! What in God's name are we *doing* out here on the high seas?' William's hollow laughter rang out across the water as they bent in unison and their boat slid weightlessly. 'Meanwhile up there in the mountains somewhere, two hundred guests will soon be gathering in all their finery.'

The setting sun passed behind a bank of clouds, and as it did, everything about them took on an inky gloom, the air chilling too, as if a cheerless god had seized the helm. All at once the towering cliff face that now rose to their right and the great body of water they moved across appeared immense and sinister, the whole enterprise freighted with folly. What tiny insignificant interlopers they were, she thought with a shiver. And all the while the light was slipping away.

In the far distance, a handsome yacht had dropped anchor for the night. Uniformed crew were serving sundowners on a silver tray to the reclining passengers. They caught the quiet clink of ice being dispensed and the low melody of polite social laughter. It was an elegant boat with sails like the rigging of one of the pirate ships that once besieged these shores. 'That's Janus Henderson,' he said in dismay. 'My largest single investor by some way. A man who likes to wine and dine the great and the good. Please God, let him not glance this way.' William averted his face and leant into his oar, so that they had soon left the boat far behind. Alice glanced at the sun as it dropped ever nearer the horizon, thinking with foreboding of the depths of darkness that night-time would soon bring.

Mary got the children into their night clothes before settling them in front of a cartoon on their iPad, and hastening to unwrap the bed linen in the laundry-room. It had been stacked in boxes almost to the ceiling for some days now. The caterer was in a panic. They urgently needed as much floor space as possible, the woman had gabbled at her, before rushing off again. But Mary's heaviness of heart slowed her. Beaufort Bed Linen. *We don't just dream of a better world, we're setting out to create one.* Each box yielded an assortment of wrapped packages. Stiff squares of 1500 thread count sheets and pillowcases folded around cardboard and swathed in cellophane, together with several great pillowy duck down and feather mattress toppers – *enrapture becomes the new norm* – each of which expanded like a conjuring trick once released from their zippered confinement. The clean smell of new cotton filled the air as she worked, methodically setting the wrapping to one side, which soon rose higher than the linen it had swaddled. Even after the best efforts of the laundry press, the linen would never again possess this origami-like precision and usually she cherished the exquisite order as she set the sheets in precise rows on the shelves. But today she worked on automatic pilot, thinking only of how she would break the news to Angel and every now and then taking out a tissue to impatiently wipe away the wetness pooling in the bottom of her glasses.

Already the caterer's assistants were beginning to fill the newly available space. *'Deprisa, deprisa!'* one of them urged her. 'First guests are arriving. It's show time, baby!' The relays of assistants carrying plastic storage boxes hurried in and out of the room, bumping and skirting around one another, parrying jokes in rapid Spanish. As Mary unwrapped the last package, the bedding company's invoice fell to the floor with a small *thunk*. She picked it up, thinking madam would want it for her records, and smoothed it flat. As she did so, her eye was caught by the total printed in bold. A figure a little less than half her annual salary. She checked it several times as she waited for the dizzying whistle in her ears to pass. It wasn't shock exactly. Neither did she feel any particular rancour. More a disorientation at the unfathomable mystery of God's plan.

'OK.' Alice came to an abrupt decision, lifting her oar clear of the water and allowing the boat to drift. For a moment the sun was no more than a sliver balanced on the horizon. And then in the wink of an eye it had dropped from view, leaving no more than a wash of peach afterglow to mark its passing. 'I hate to say this. But. Realistically. We're going to have to head to shore. Make a camp. Resume in the morning.'

Make a camp. William closed his eyes and exhaled. He no sooner knew how to 'make a camp' than he would know how to fly to the moon. Hearing the faint put-putting of a distant fishing boat, his eyes snapped open again. Two fishermen at the helm of a traditional wooden *llaüt*, also heading south. Plan B appearing – just like that! *There was a God after all.*

'Help! *Socorro!*' Willian half raised himself in his seat, waving his oar aloft. Catching his faint cry, one of the men looked around, before nudging his companion, and now both men had turned.

In his mind's eye William retrieved the linen shirt. Re-poured the snifter of whisky, this time as a celebratory triple shot. He settled back into his seat to await rescue. *Eventually, just as we had given up hope and were resigning ourselves to a night under the stars, two fishermen hauled us to safety.*

But instead of turning the tiller, one of the men was rising to his feet and slowly rolling up his right shirtsleeve with a careful deliberation. What on earth was he doing? William strained to discern his purpose in the twilight, watching as the man made a tight fist with his right hand before raising it in the air as he slapped his bicep with the other hand in the age-old gesture of obscenity. Then he sat down again and spat into the sea before turning back to resume his southward journey. The sound of the men's guttural laughter came in fragments on the wind.

Only moments later, their kayak was abruptly rocked

from side to side as if the cheerless God were now giving the pair an impatient shake. William held the sides as their kayak rose and fell on the fishing boat's departing wake. He listened to the slap slap of agitated waves hitting their prow. Slap, slap. The lobster fisherman's revenge. Slap, slap. Alice's silence was so deafening he daren't even glance her way. *What on earth had he been thinking when he passed by on the other side of the road like that?* They rose and fell, until the wake finally dispersed away in ever widening circles, allowing their boat to settle again.

Without further discussion, they turned for the coastline and in a short while had reached the shore. Then, with his arm about Alice, William hefted himself up and out of the boat. They limped across the beach together before stepping into the shadowed forest and beginning to ascend the steep incline. Only the faintest outline of things remained. Something that might have been an owl passed close over their heads, flying so slowly it appeared weighted by the improbable length of its own wingspan. And little by little the scutterings of invisible night creatures filled the darkness. They hadn't climbed for long before they came to the shadowed frame of a half-finished building, wispy pine saplings sprouting through its roofless rooms.

'This'll do,' Alice said, sliding from under his shoulder and looking about. They weren't the first people to have taken refuge here, since the breeze-block walls were garlanded with graffiti, still just discernible in the last of the light, and someone had set a dilapidated old sofa and two plastic sunloungers in a circle around the blackened remnants of a campfire.

'Age before beauty,' Alice said, gesturing at the sofa. 'Sit, rest your weary bones. I'll make a fire so we can at least see what we're doing.'

William pressed an exploratory hand against the grubby sofa base before letting his knees collapse beneath him, welcoming its assenting give despite the sweet mushroom stench of mildew it exuded. The humidity of the windless summer evening induced an almost instantaneous weariness. It was the kind of clammy warmth that drew mosquitoes. The kind that those thermostatic power showers were so effective at remedying. It was about now he'd usually go in search of something delicious from the cellar, before ceremonially savouring it in one of his fine Riedel wine glasses. He could just make out Alice moving between the trees, gathering firewood. Mary would be turning the beds down, before switching on the air con. He recalled with a faint pang that cool slipstream as the first wafts of cold began to override the humid evening air. Remembered the sensual glide of Egyptian cotton as he slid into bed at the end of the day.

Bone weary, he watched Alice kneeling to construct a small tepee of wood in the makeshift hearth before taking out her lighter. As the kindling flared into life she sat down on the battered sunlounger opposite him and they both watched the blaze catch as the logs became a bright crown. He caught intermittent glimpses of her pensive face as she sat apparently hypnotised by the flames. The sound of a curlew pierced the silence, its mellifluous, plaintive cry passing high overhead.

'If this is all a dream, it's an astonishingly well-sustained one,' he said at length.

Alice lay down and shifted about for a while, until she eventually settled. It was difficult to be sure, but in the flickering half-light William got the impression she had closed her eyes. He observed her for some while. How familiar and yet how other she remained.

He sat lost in the wash of bittersweet memory. He had simply to direct his mind there to remember it all as if it were yesterday. The thing between him and Jess had all kicked off in that little beach *chiringuito* with sand underfoot and stars overhead. He remembered that after the gathering of old friends at the dinner on that first night, in the confusion of so many people being dispatched to their hotel, they had both drunkenly climbed into the same taxi from different sides, only to collide on the back seat. He could still recall how his heart had jackknifed at their unexpected proximity.

'Well, hello there.' Her firm grip prevented his panic-stricken attempt to slide away. 'Must be ten years at least . . . I miss our little spats. Not many people were brave enough to take me on like that.' He had stammered something about how this must be his lucky night, knowing it was a lame line even as he offered it, but too undone by the press of her bare thigh against his to improve on it. The realisation that he was now the sole focus of her predatory charm was like inhaling crack cocaine. How astonishing and delicious it was that her hand should now be moving from his arm to his flies, every hair follicle alive to her lightly skimming fingertips.

As the forward momentum of the cab slid them backwards in their seat, he remembered turning to her in the darkness as she undid his belt – stunned by this new possibility opening between them.

'I thought you were a married woman now . . .'

'Not tonight, City Boy.'

In the dim glow of light, he saw the dainty strap of her dress had fallen from her shoulder, revealing the curve of a bare breast, and desire was upon him like a wolf, any remnants of nerves instantly vanquished. Once they arrived at the hotel, she had pretty much frog-marched him to her room, where they had spent the rest of that weekend in what could only be described as a joyous derangement. The necessity of avoiding being caught together by any of their mutual friends billeted in the same hotel, together with the knowledge they would shortly be flying home to their respective partners, simply served to heighten the piquancy of their derangement. He saw again the dishes from room service piling up by the door. Momentarily savoured the vivid recollection of an elated and naked nocturnal swim in the hotel pool. It was as if they were sharing a last huzzah for what little was left of their youth. And at some point, as their hours together dwindled, he had referred to Jess's husband Pete as the Yes Man and she had flown at him. Yet he had seen it as the indignation of someone who recognised an unwelcome home truth – amongst their group, he certainly wasn't the only one to think Pete unworthy of her. And it galled him that she appeared to have every intention of returning to Pete when William would have stood down his newly burgeoning relationship with Cressida in a heartbeat. But when he tried to talk to her about the kind of future they might forge together, she had only put a finger to his lips to shush him.

His ears were newly alive to the forest's subtle hums and clicks. The subterranean flow of communication between root systems, a low vibration below. Here he lay, amongst the creatures of the night. William moved about, feeling broken springs twang from deep within the sofa. Like twinges of conscience. There was something fundamental he hadn't yet shared with Alice. Something she had a right to know, and the weight of his withholding burdened him.

Guests were drifting in with the gathering dusk. They arrived in straggling groups, briefly hovering at the edge of the crowd to take stock, before plunging amongst the press of bodies and thump of music. Cressida waited at the bar for her mojito to be garnished with mint, the two she'd already consumed in such rapid succession bestowing, along with the sedative, an unusually potent effect. The evening was motoring on its own momentum and she had simply to kiss the familiar faces hello and look about her, exchanging pleasantries with a fixed smile. William had been delayed by a work crisis, she told all those who enquired. But with luck would arrive at any moment. That bit at least was true. Some way off she could see the camel chewing cud, while the handler, now dressed as a Bedouin tribesman, held its lead and posed next to the press of guests who waited to have their picture taken. Despite the fact that William wasn't here to see it, her guests' vocal pleasure at the spectacle was gratifying. It would be a small Instagram sensation tomorrow at least. *Hostest with the mostest*, she thought, lifted by a sudden soaring elation as the conjunction of chemicals moving through her veins hit a rare pharmaceutical sweet spot of optimum fusion. *Hot damn. I'll take it.*

She downed her mojito in one before tripping sideways on her absurdly high heels, which somehow loosened her fingers from about the slender stem of her cocktail glass. Certainly, shards of glass were now crunching underfoot as she stumbled sideways. A man caught her and brought her upright again.

'Cress – is everything – are you . . .?' The features of the man coalesced into those of Marcus. *Darling Marcus. Her knight in shining armour.* She recalled a brief but thrilling kiss at a party in Suffolk many years ago now. They had been interrupted, but a low-level frisson had come and gone between them ever since. Now here was an opportunity for closure. Yet as she attempted to draw him towards her, she was confused to find he was instead pulling away.

'Whoah there, Cress,' he was saying. 'Let's get you a shot of black coffee, shall we?' He was waving at one of the waiters.

She was dimly aware of staff materialising from amongst the crowds to sweep the broken glass away, of someone else putting a new cocktail in her hand and the next thing Marcus had vanished again and the momentum of the crowd was carrying her on towards the dance floor. She collided with a woman who was dancing on her toes like a high-spirited pony. Beside her a man in a kaftan twirled his hands towards the skies, apparently in the grip of a religious visitation. Sequinned dresses glittered and caught the light as their wearers bumped and weaved, and Cressida allowed herself to be taken up by the music too, submitting to the delicious imperative of the bass line.

William emerged from his reverie with a start, becoming aware that Alice had opened her eyes again and was once more staring into the fire. He set his feet back on the ground, drew in a deep breath, and leant forward. Cleared his throat. Planted a damp palm on each knee. Cleared his throat again.

'Look. I feel it's only right I tell you. You and I have actually met before. Though you were so small you might argue it barely constituted a meeting. About two years after the Ibiza weekend, Jess and I met for lunch. Only to my surprise she brought you along too in a pushchair. I just assumed she wanted to rub my face in the fruits of her relationship with Pete. And then halfway through the lunch, she rather casually dropped the bombshell that it was me, not Pete, who was your biological father.'

Alice sat absorbing this, saying nothing. The long silence that ensued between them was filled with more whirrings of the night. The barking of dogs echoed across the mountain before passing away as their cries were taken up by more dogs further down the valley, like a canine call and response moving in an auditory Mexican wave around the island. He waited in an agonised state of suspense for her to respond.

From the darkness came a different noise now; a snatch of someone shouting exultantly in Spanish, peals of wild laughter, a mocking splinter of song. Then three firecrackers in quick succession, like gunshots in the night. Followed by spiralling pink plumes of flames that burst above their heads in a bright flower of falling fire. It came to him that the locals were celebrating the summer solstice. Of course. They would be partying in Sant Joan. *The end of something old. The start of something new.* How very apt. And then, the lurching and unwelcome recollection of his birthday party. Were all those guests really even now gathered to toast a man who wasn't there?

'Right,' she said at last, and as she spoke, the largest log on the bonfire broke open, exposing the dark fiery interior, causing sparks to explode upwards like bright moths whirring into the darkness. 'So if you've known about me all along, why the hell did you never get in touch?'

The noise of the party was beginning to ratchet up like an engine gathering speed as the roar of voices competed to be heard over the music. Mary had been instructed to walk about with a tray of drinks, but there were so many other waiting staff whisking through the crowds with their laden trays held aloft, it hardly seemed to matter whether she did or not. Every now and then she had to set the tray down to noisily blow her nose and dab her eyes.

Even at the best of times an evening like this was an ordeal for her. It was always unsettling to observe the *banyaga* avidly down their firewater with such alacrity. On such a scale, you couldn't but fail to observe the group unravelling as the glassy eyes began to look more inward than out – and the gales of laughter grow wilder and less expressive of any real amusement. Here was the true nature of godless people laid bare. She passed the stall serving trays of sushi. Another with bite-sized tapas treats. Hands kept reaching out from the shadows to snatch up the cocktails from her tray and after replenishing her supply several times, she walked about collecting the empty glasses instead. Tonight, her invisibility amongst so many felt all at once amplified into something darkly liberating – as if all personal accountability could be temporarily suspended. Imagine if you took this opportunity to redistribute a little of the abundance on display according to need. No one would suffer. Or even necessarily notice . . . And even if they did, how would they ever know who to hold accountable? She hastened her step.

From the first-floor corridor, the sound of laughter and the thump of music was no more than a distant disturbance. She tapped at the door, before stepping smartly into Kate and Marcus's bedroom, smoothing down the counterpane as she passed, play-acting a bona fide housekeeping visit – for whose benefit, she hadn't the least idea. The sharp rat-tat-tat at the window made her spin about in panic. Throughout her childhood, like all Filipino children, she'd been warned about the Wakwak, a vampiric bird-like creature that came to snatch people at night. It was hard to be sure whether the movement outside was a Wakwak ruffling its plumage or merely branches shifting in the wind, but then she heard the creature speak in the dialect of her village, its high-pitched voice muffled by the glass. 'What naughtiness are you up to, little Mahalic?' She barely managed to stifle her cry of terror before wrenching the curtains closed, and standing for a moment with her hand over her heart, feeling its contraction.

Then she was in the bathroom, with the jewellery box opening of its own accord on its expensive hinges and that discreet ring somehow plucked from amongst its more ostentatious companions to lie cupped in the palm of her hand, its modest weight so puzzlingly countered by its potential market value. She slid it quickly into her pocket, as if gulping something down. Then found herself smoothly descending the stairs, powered by her still pounding heart, and back amongst the noisy press of people, too dazed to feel anything other than an echo of shock that kept rushing upon her as she picked up her tray again. But no one so much as glanced in her direction other than to return their empty glasses, until her tray was soon full again. She passed two other Filipino women, friends from church she had recruited for the night, standing with mops at the fringes of the crowd, ready to hasten forward and wipe up any spillages, and all at once she felt feather light, already airborne and on her way to the Philippines.

The crackle and fizz of a new volley of fireworks coincided with the abrupt muting of the sound system. Someone clapped their hands and the faces of two hundred guests turned towards Cressida in the ensuing silence.

'Ah. So. Hello. Good evening. Thank you all so much for coming. And. I want to say how sorry I am that William hasn't been able to make it, after all.' She looked about at the shadowed faces. 'The truth is we haven't really been . . .' An ear-piercing shriek of feedback cut the air. She took a deep breath. 'He . . . Well we . . .' She became aware of Kate's restraining hand on her arm. 'Well, let's just say he can be a bit of a law unto himself – as many of you will know. But if you happen to see him . . . Send him home, will you?'

The low uncertain laughter tailed away into an embarrassed silence. A clatter of distant glasses being stacked by the bar staff. People looking at their feet. Kate stepped up beside her, turning to the guests with a game smile.

'Ladies and gentleman, please raise your glasses. To William. *In absentia.*'

'To William,' the guests echoed, though there was an upward inflexion that suggested it was as much a question as a dedication. And then, as if by divine intervention, the DJ put on a new track and all tension was expelled in a burst of renewed noise and laughter.

'Well done,' Kate said low in her ear.

But Cressida had seized Kate's hand in hers and was drawing her towards the car park as the fireworks resumed their deafening crescendo overhead, illuminating the entire night sky in a new spangled waterfall of light. 'Come,' she said. 'Want to show you something.'

For a moment, the ricocheting explosion of the fireworks precluded any further conversation, the shower of falling light momentarily illuminating their small encampment.

William waited until the peace of the night had been restored. Doubting he could trust his voice, he began experimentally. 'When word reached me on the grapevine that Jess had had a child, it simply never crossed my mind it might be mine. So when she broke the news that it was actually me who was your biological father, I was completely blindsided. I asked her how she wanted to proceed. And she was adamant that Pete understood the situation and would raise you as his own. That he doted on you. She was absolutely determined that nothing need change. Wouldn't even hear of me making a financial contribution.' He gestured helplessly. 'What could I do, Alice? I felt I had no choice but to respect her wishes. To stake any kind of parental claim against Jess's explicit wishes would only have been to destroy the security of your world . . . And so that lunch was actually the last time I saw either of you.'

Afterwards he had always looked back on this abrupt revelation of paternity as one of those exceedingly rare events when a fine membrane breaks and from one moment to the next you are on the instant no longer the person you were. When a prolonged, and some would surely have said overextended, boyhood slipped from his shoulders. There were responsibilities and allegiances he wanted to offer this Lilliputian creature. Issues of accountability. Ancestry. His head had swum with the sheer momentousness of it all.

The ensuing months had passed in shades of grey. He'd licked his wounds and lain low. Told no one. The abrupt revelation of himself as a father was too dizzying and strange to frame in words, and anyway – who could he tell? It was far too incendiary a fact to share with those who knew them. He often wondered if Jess had come to the lunch with the intention of telling him, or the wine had simply loosened her tongue.

Having always been so casual about Cressida, he surprised everyone, most particularly himself, by proposing to her. Somehow the fact she was a woman over whom he could hold sway offered his bruised ego a little solace. Even if her failure to match Jess had been something he had, in some unarticulated way, held against her ever since. Word sometimes reached him in the years that followed: Jess was teaching International Development at UEA; Jess had set up a not-for-profit foundation for street children in Brazil; Jess and Pete had jacked it all in to go travelling through Asia. Friends rolled their eyes fondly, caught between admiration and disapproval at their freewheeling life with a small child in tow.

'You may find this hard to understand or to forgive. I get that. But it wasn't easy. Every now and then, something would unexpectedly ambush me. I'd see a father in the park playing with his kid. Or Cressida would badger me that it was time to start our own family. In the wee small hours of the night I'd remind myself of Jess's assurance that Pete was a doting father. And then, at some point, I heard she'd been diagnosed with breast cancer.'

He could just make out the glitter of Alice's eyes as she listened.

'When I heard the news about her illness, it never crossed my mind that she wouldn't make it. It sounds so ridiculously naive now, I know. But she was still young, still so full of zest. How could anything quench such a spirit? And I was several drafts into a carefully worded email wishing her the speediest of recoveries and wondering if we might perhaps meet again, when a mutual friend rang to tell me she had died.'

Such a pall of sadness and regret had fallen across the entire chapter that he had ring-fenced it all in some hinterland of his mind. That was the extraordinary thing he couldn't now fathom. That he had managed to know and not know.

He recalled the rising panic every time Cressida attempted to lobby him about starting a family. It wasn't an issue he could bear to discuss. So she'd gone ahead and taken the choice from him. After Lola and then Joe came along, meeting their demands, together with the pressures of his professional life, had forced Alice's existence ever further to the darkest, most forbidden recesses of his mind. What a curious thing. To have three children and yet not have consented to a single one.

Alice sat silently, taking it all in. Then she laid down again. At length her voice came from the darkness. 'It's all just so incredibly sad.'

He lay back and made a pillow for his head with his hands as he considered how best to answer, exhaustion moving through him, forcing his eyes to keep closing. He adjusted his weight, trying to locate the soft spots in the sagging sofa, failing to suppress a loud yawn. 'Yet here you are, Alice. How can I possibly regret a thing?' Another yawn broke from him, wide enough to make his jaw ache. 'But right now, if you'll forgive me, all that walking has completely done me in.' He continued to shift about for a bit, before finally settling. 'Let the wild animals devour me,' he muttered, before sleep closed over him.

Soon a gigglingly inebriated group had crammed themselves into Rene's pick-up truck with one of the security team hired for the evening at the wheel. The night air that streamed through the open air was pungent with baked plant life. Somehow there was still a half-full margarita in Cressida's hand and in the other the cigarette she had retrieved from her clutch bag. Someone had lit it for her and she held it out of the open window with an elegant insouciance, until the slipstream of air drew it from between her fingers and bounced it away through the darkness, leaving a trail of tiny orange sparks as it flew, before vanishing into the parched undergrowth at the side of the road. She leant forward to turn the music up, before blowing out her last exhalation of smoke and downing the remainder of the margarita in one.

The sturdy flanks of the Sant Joan church had become the canvas for a revolving light projection that depicted engravings from Ibiza's past: a peasant woman in traditional dress holding a lamb in her arms, and then the serene face of the goddess Tanit flickering over the plaster walls, larger-than-life images of a lost pastoral life whose scale dwarfed the festive press of people passing to and fro along the main street.

The church bells were striking midnight as Cressida, swinging her arms with a drunken elan, hastened her guests on through the teeming crowds. They entered the small piazza, which was packed with dancing revellers, at the centre a DJ spinning discs in an illuminated booth, while professional dancers gyrated on oiled hips, twirling blazing fire sticks that flared rhythmically above the heads of the crowd. A towering figure on stilts, wearing a long shroud and a giant papier-mâché head of Tanit, blocked her way. Every time Cressida tried to sidestep her, the figure moved with her, mirroring Cressida's alarmed motions with such accuracy that passers-by broke into laughter. Then the figure receded into the shadows with a graceful genuflection of her giant papier-mâché head, allowing Cressida to hurry her guests onwards again towards the distant thunder of African drums.

They arrived at the edges of the field just as the last bonfire was being lit. The line of onlookers were illuminated by the golden blaze of the fires, raised phones held aloft to record the scene. The pyres of logs caught quickly, producing a thick white smoke that billowed about their ankles. Then, at a given signal, the shadowed figures of revellers, either singly or hand in hand, or sometimes with a small child in their arms, began to jump the fires one after the other, while the watching crowds shouted and whistled their encouragement and the thundering of drums surged in velocity.

Cressida clapped along with them, the heat from the fires coming in intermittent gusts on the evening air. Another gust made the smoke sting her eyes and red embers hop and bounce about her feet. The whoops, and whistles, the drums, then the distant artillery noise of firecrackers ricocheting was like a primal call to arms. *The end of something old, the start of something new.* On an impulse, she pushed to the front of the queue and, kicking off her absurdly high heels, hitched her silk dress about her hips.

'Oh God. I can't look,' Charlie covered his eyes. 'This can only end in tears.'

Kate hurried forward to try and restrain her but Cressida was already leaping the first fire before staggering sideways. Then recovering, she jumped each of the remaining fifteen bonfires in turn, before coming to an unsteady halt and raising a victorious fist. At which, one after the other, her gawping guests broke into an admiring and faintly astonished round of applause.

Alice took in William's sleeping form, noting how his legs overspilled the end of the sofa. All those times she pushed away her puzzlement at how she could be so tall while Pete was so short. All those times she had been unsettled by Pete's declarations of gratitude that she should have been 'sent to him' – how the oddness of the phrase had troubled her in a way that never made any sense since the sentiment was so clearly intended to be loving. A myriad tiny clues she had chosen not to dwell on.

When Pete confessed the whole thing, he had been at pains to emphasise that it had been Jess's wish to keep the truth from her only until she was old enough to deal with it. That he genuinely couldn't have loved her more, regardless of whether they shared common blood or not. She saw that both men had acted with what they believed to be the most honourable of intentions. That it had not been a situation of either of their making.

From the depths of the night came the shifting melancholy weight and movement of sea, and there was the moon, appearing above the horizon like a ghostly nocturnal inversion of the sun that had only so recently set there, its milky light illuminating the slow progression of clouds that moved across it.

On the edge of sleep now, an impression of her mother came to her, glimpsed as if from the periphery of memory. A certain playfulness perhaps. A tenderness of tone. She had grown up revering her mother's memory. Yet how could Jess not have considered the complexity her insistence on secrecy would bequeath on those closest to her? If Jess's high-minded principles on the big political issues of her day had always lent her a mythic quality, this insistence on duplicity suggested a rather more puzzling myopia on issues of the heart.

Alice would go home and face the music. She could be on the ferry to Barcelona by midmorning tomorrow. And. A new possibility came to her. And perhaps after the trial she might return here – if all went well – and simply slip below the radar. She had always dreamt of finding work on a farm. Paloma came to her in a jangle of bracelets and she cursed herself for not taking her number.

She knew the sky blazed with stars, but she felt too lightly attached to the earth to risk looking at them. Instead she closed her eyes and willed sleep to take her.

'Mummy.' A hoarse voice in the darkness.

Cressida could just make out Lola's diminutive outline. Cressida's mouth was as dry as sandpaper and the blessed anaesthesia the alcohol and Xanax had bestowed was now superseded by a terrible thirst and the residual sensation of having fatally poisoned herself. She became aware of the acrid scent of woodsmoke in her hair. And – then – dear God – fractured memories of the night. The humiliating absence of William. The horrible suspicion she had almost certainly made a complete spectacle of herself.

'Did you have a bad dream, sweetheart?'

A suppressed hiccup of assenting tears. She pulled her daughter to her, as she had done many times before when Lola came seeking refuge from night terrors. Sleep was just drawing her into its warm embrace when Lola's tear-choked voice came again like a tiny blowtorch in her ear.

'I want my bedroom back.'

'Sweetie.' Alice was just visiting, I promise you. And now she's gone again.'

The child settled against her, as hot as oven-warmed bread, and Cressida stroked her hair, listening to her breath lengthen until Lola had slipped with remarkable rapidity back into sleep. Just like her father – as if a shutter had fallen.

Now wide awake and too hung-over for sleep to ever be a possibility, Cressida stretched an exploratory leg backwards into the space beside her, just in case William had crept in under cover of darkness. But her foot moved without impediment across the empty slipperiness of sheet. No softly snoring husband tonight. Where could he be? She would kill him. If he ever came back. If his body wasn't already floating face down in the sea. No – instead of killing him, actually she would divorce him. She would use the redundancy money she had squirrelled away to instruct the best divorce lawyer she could afford. She was clear about that now. And before she divorced him, she would give him the kind of dressing down she should have done years ago. If she were advising a friend in this situation, what would she tell them? A fierce conviction rose in her as she formulated a potential road map on behalf of this theoretical friend. She would probably urge them to get a qualification in something practical. To regain agency at all costs and reclaim the independent woman they had somehow lost along the way. As she lay turning it all over, the first glimmer of light began to appear about the edges of the curtain.

4

Alice woke to the same faint glow of dawn and went down to survey the sea. Once the tip of the sun lit the horizon, she hurried back to wake William. Even as he was stumbling to his feet, the sky was moving with such rapidity from night to day, it was as if they were being thrust back through a portal, the desolate lone calls of the night birds swiftly giving way to the gregarious chatter of their daylight cousins as the warming earth began to give up its familiar smell of aniseed and curry.

William waited in a daze for Alice to gather her things and stamp with care on the charred remains of the fire. In the breaking daylight she could just make out a line of electricity pylons cutting through the dense tree cover further up the hill.

She examined him. Underneath the dried mud that still streaked his face, a salt and pepper stubble had sprouted about his jawline, and though she reached out several times to smooth down his hair, it kept springing back again in wild disarray.

'Ready?'

'Ready.' He rubbed his eyes.

'Rested?' He made a humphing sound. 'Come on then, old man.'

With his arm once more across her shoulder, she drew him up the hill, following the pylons, which eventually brought them to the edge of an asphalt road that dissected the forest.

'I can't believe this,' William said, looking to left and right in confusion at the road as it ran in either direction like an unfurling ribbon of tar. 'It really felt like we were a million miles from civilisation last night!'

It was only after she had set the table for twenty, juiced a small sack of oranges and was on her way back from the chicken coop with a basket of fresh eggs that Mary first noticed it.

The early morning sky as it lightened beyond the hill was subtly infused either with grey cloud vapour or – a faint haze of smoke. As she stood rooted to the spot, trying to decide which of the two it might be, the drone of a small plane passed low overhead.

'Uh-oh,' Marcus said, glancing skywards as he passed by on his way to the pool, a towel slung over one shoulder. 'Sounds a bit ominous. Isn't that a fire plane?'

Mary had feared her punishment would come. But in her worst nightmares she hadn't anticipated it being on such a scale.

Upon the wicked he shall rain snares, fire and brimstone and burning wind will be the portion of the cup.

She watched the plane vanish over the brow of the hill towards the smoke, before dropping the basket of eggs and starting to run, shouting as she went,

'Madam, madam! Wake up! Wake up!'

William and Alice inched their way arm in arm along the grass verge, the heat of the day already making itself felt despite the earliness of the hour. The warming air brought with it the sharp tang of petrochemicals rising up from the recently resurfaced road. Hearing the low purr of an approaching engine, Alice raised her thumb, squinting as the rising sun broke in dazzling mote-filled slats through the trees. When the car came into sight, a heat haze had blurred its contours into free-floating slivers that coalesced into the sleek contours of a BMW as it slid to a halt beside them like a gleaming chariot.

The electric window opened to reveal a handsome and sun-tanned driver, who surveyed them both with an incredulous expression. 'Boy, oh boy. Must have been quite a party!' The man let out a low whistle, glancing at the woman beside him for affirmation, but she had turned her head away with a sulky expression and folded her arms. He glanced doubtfully over one shoulder at the pristine seats of his car. Then, perhaps eager for someone to buffer the onerous company of his bad-tempered companion, inclined his head anyway. *Get in.*

The air was lightly chilled as they slid across the soft leather of the back seats. In profile, the woman's lips were improbably augmented and her minute crocheted dress struggled to contain surgically enhanced bosoms whose rounded contours rose like a flotation system. She forced the edges of her swollen mouth upwards, glancing over one shoulder with a moue that was at once bored and disdainful, before flicking back her acrylic blond hair extensions with a sigh of discontent. She was as close to a living cartoon as Alice had ever set eyes on. In fact, both the man and the woman had an unnervingly synthetic quality, like facsimiles of human beings dreamt up by an overzealous product designer.

The car took off again with all the velocity of an earthbound rocket and, detached from all scents and sounds, the countryside slipped past the window with a dreamlike unreality. Alice sat balanced on the edge of her seat, but William was settling back against the luxurious leather upholstery, taking in the different screens on a dashboard more akin to a flight deck. On the screen they were a flying arrow advancing along a grey vertical stripe with blocks of synthetic green to indicate the countryside through which they sped. He patted Alice's hand, turning to smile in comradely acknowledgement of the shared lunacy of their escapade, before tipping his head back against the ergonomically constructed headrest, exhaling with a chuckle.

'I know this might be hard to believe,' he said to the driver. 'But we were out walking yesterday and got so lost, we ended up having to spend the night in the woods!'

The man was glancing between them in the rear-view mirror. He shook his head. 'How can you possibly get lost on such a small island?' He spoke with the faintest of Israeli accents.

'Trust me. I've asked myself that very question many times over the past twenty-four hours. As my wife doubtless will too, once I'm home.'

'Guess you won't have heard about the fire, then?' The man looked over his shoulder, holding the wheel with a possessive ease.

'Fire.' William sat bolt upright again. 'What fire?'

'Somewhere up near Sant Vicent, apparently.'

'Christ. My house, my whole family are in Sant Vicent . . .'

William passed a hand through his knotted hair, taking this in as the road rushed towards them. He asked to borrow the phone and the man unclipped it, handing it to him over one shoulder. He dialled rapidly, cursing under his breath as each new attempt failed to make a connection.

'Sounds like the telephone masts have gone down, my friend.' The road dipped and rose as it traced the curves of the valley.

'Can you take me to my car? I left it in the middle of nowhere – about halfway between Sant Vicent and Sant Carles.'

'That's not exactly on my way – but guess it would be a little heartless to throw you out in the middle of nowhere again.'

William leant forward as if to lend extra momentum to the car's trajectory. 'Please hurry.'

The woman read out news updates on her phone in a densely rolling Russian accent as they sped northwards. The fact that William's family might be implicated in an unfolding drama appeared to have roused her from her bad humour. The authorities had sent for more firefighting planes from Barcelona, she read. And now the police were evacuating everyone within a two-kilometre radius of the fire. Alice squeezed his hand.

'What about you?' he said, turning to her with a start. 'We need to get you to the port . . .'

'I'll work something out.'

As they drew nearer, William prayed he would remember the route he had taken. 'It feels like a lifetime ago,' he said. He craned his head, issuing instructions at each new turning, until at last they had miraculously arrived beside his jeep again. He leant down and took the keys from under the hub of the front tyre while Alice recovered his phone from its holder on the dashboard. She raised a gesture of farewell to the Israeli man and his companion as William started up the car and hit the rutted track with his foot flat to the floor.

It wasn't until they turned onto the road to the house that they saw the first real rolling plumes of dark smoke that billowed up from behind the hill. Churning clouds so voluminous and dense they could only be produced by fire of an immense scale. Every now and then a few bright flames flared along the treeline, before vanishing again.

Around the next corner their progress was halted by a police blockade manned by two Guardia Civil. The larger of the two came forward, gesturing for them to turn around and go back the way they had come.

'Tell him I need to get to my house.'

But when Alice translated, the officer shook his head. 'Dice que no es posible porque es demasiado peligroso.'

'He's saying it's too dangerous.'

'Tell him everything I own is in that house.'

The policeman regarded them with a sceptical expression, glancing towards his colleague, as Alice translated again. She pressed her hands together in a gesture of entreaty. At this the smaller colleague reluctantly nodded, while the larger man held up his extended palm, five fingers splayed for emphasis.

'OK, Señor – five minutes. You have five minutes. No more.'

Coming abreast of a break in the trees, they slowed to survey the vista it revealed. A long line of brilliant orange flames consumed the forest with a fierce merriment, momentarily solarising each new tree before leaving in its wake only withered stumps in a blackened wasteland.

Alice watched a convoy of fire planes appear through the swirling smoke, each taking it in turns to tip their trailing container of seawater onto the flames, so that the water billowed in a slow-motion cascade. The upward leap of flames and the darting airborne efforts of the little planes to douse them appeared hopelessly mismatched. *The natural world was evicting them.* She felt it in her very bones and sinew as the stench of burning came gusting on the wind towards them.

As they sped up the drive, he pressed the remote control to open the gates and tried to prepare himself for what they might find. Yet, as the gates glided open, apart from the billowing smoke, everything looked exactly as he had left it. They got out of the jeep, looking about them, listening to how close the roar and snap of the fire sounded, the exceptional dryness of the forest apparent in the continual crack of collapsing wood. There was a total absence of birdsong and even the incessant whirring of the cicadas had ceased. The plumes of smoke were curling towards them down the hillside, as if to show the fire the way. Unless the wind changed direction very soon, the whole place would be done for.

Once – not so long ago – he had believed that in this place resided the repository of everything that was William Gifford. Yet, though he sought in vain for a coherent plan of action, he could get no purchase on what to do now, his thoughts slipping and colliding. So many plans and decisions had made this land and house his. Such a deep investment of time and heart.

He became aware that Alice was guiding him towards the front door. He looked on as she grappled with the handle, before spinning about with an urgent expression of enquiry. He could only gesture helplessly. *No key.* He became aware his face was wet with tears. *Good God. Get a grip man. Get a grip.*

He watched as Alice picked up one of the garden chairs and swung it against a window, turning her face from the cascade of tinkling glass, before knocking out the remaining shards with her shoe and climbing in. Moments later she had thrown the door open and William was stumbling into the house behind her. Was the roar and crackle of flames really growing louder? He imagined it encircling the house. Imagined them entombed. They were both coughing in unison now, choking on the acrid reek of carbon. *What on earth was it he had come for?* From a great distance, he felt Alice's hand on his arm and heard her speak in a calm undertone.

'Passports. Bank cards. Prioritise.'

In his study, he took out the hidden key and threw open the safe. But fear had emptied his mind. Then Alice was at his elbow again, shovelling all the documents and wallet into an envelope, and manoeuvring him to the front door with a tender authority that touched him. Even in the midst of his terror he was moved beyond words.

Outside, he tried to stifle small cries of grief as the black cinders fell twirling about them like some strange unholy inversion of snow.

'Let's go, let's go.' Alice was pulling and pushing him.

Overhead a new and deafening roar. A helicopter swooping so low its thunderous cacophony forced them to clap their hands to their ears. The tops of the palm trees swayed crazily in the slipstream of air from its propeller and he watched its cradle of water swing on its long chain, before its contents drenched first the flank of the house, the water falling sideways, before drenching them too. The awning of the marquee had half collapsed under the weight of water. Only one last section stood, ballooning under its burden of liquid.

As they stepped out through the gates, the smoke was so dense, the road was barely visible. But through the haze came figure after figure heading downhill to Sant Joan. A man herding three goats, behind him a family of five pulling suitcases on wheels. As William and Alice fell in behind them they came abreast of two girls leading a line of horses, every now and then stopping to wrestle with one or other as the terrified creatures danced at the edge of anarchy. A small child just ahead of them on the road stumbled and fell and the mother, encumbered by the baby and bags in her arms, struggled in vain to help her up. Seeing their distress, Alice lifted up the child and William took the mother's bags from her, dragging them behind him as he limped.

They kept moving with the slow crocodile of people until the commotion of the helicopters and smoke had been left behind. As they reached the police cordon again, a news crew now stood filming the procession of people. What strange topsy-turvy new world order was this in which they were no longer observing these scenes of exodus from the comfort of their armchairs but had somehow become the on-screen refugees? He would have raised a hand to screen his face, but the heavy bags prevented him.

Here they all were fleeing their homes together – the hippies from their hidden places, the Ibicencos who had worked the land for generations and the one-percenters who were buying it from them. All the takers and the givers. The healers, dealers and dreamers. The consumers and the conservers. The disparate now indissoluble. How nonsensical it had been to only tend his own patch so assiduously. As the buildings of Sant Joan came into sight, the habitual brilliance of a summer's day began to reassert itself in all its dazzling normality. The swirl of displaced people now thronged about the car park, where volunteers had set up a water station. He found a quiet spot under a tree for the woman and her children to take shelter while Alice went to get them something to drink. He limped on through the melee of people, trying to take it all in.

'Daddy!' A whirling commotion running at full pelt through the crowds towards him, crashing against him as first his son and then his daughter wrapped themselves about his legs. William dropped to one knee, his heart contracting with relief – he felt the very elasticity of its response.

'There was a fire,' they were both shouting in gleeful unison. 'The police said we had to leave. And Mummy told them we wouldn't – but they had guns, Daddy! Real guns. Bang, bang!'

He almost toppled under their combined weight in his arms. And then, there was Cressida bringing up the rear.

'And just where the fuck have you been?'

He tried to embrace her, but she held herself in rigid resistance. House guests were gathering about them. He tried to imagine how he must appear to them. A grubby, barefooted man returning in nothing but a pair of ragged shorts. Kate came forward to stand on tiptoes and draw a few twigs from his hair, before trying to wipe away the last remnants of soil from his face.

'Mary and Rene have done a runner,' she whispered low in his ear so the children wouldn't hear. 'Raised the alarm and then just vanished into thin air.'

He looked up at the sky, where a thin plane trail hung along the horizon, as if an artist had dabbled their brush in a pale wash of radiant white. A plane was moving at speed towards the mainland. He imagined Mary and Rene on their way to Madrid and from there the long flight to the Philippines.

Cressida was gathering up the children. 'I'm going take the kids back to the UK. I'll forward you an address when I have one. Guess we're gonna both need a solicitor.'

He was nodding in jerky assent. One life closing. The future as yet a foreign country. An ice-cold hand clutched his heart. Something he had been carefully safeguarding was somehow no longer in his possession. That emptiness beneath one arm. At some point en route he must have dropped the envelope containing his documents and wallet. He surveyed the anxious faces.

'Any chance someone could stand me breakfast?' he asked, pulling the lining of his pockets out so that they hung forlornly.

Mary looked down as the island passed beneath their plane. From here she could just see the western coastline tipping into view. She held her breath as they banked over Sant Joan, taking in the vast blackened wasteland that encircled the village. She saw how close the line of bright flames now crept towards William and Cressida's house. Saw how the tiny silhouettes of firefighters bore down on the advancing flames with their hoses. How people streamed like ants along the highways and byways, to converge in a long line on the road into Sant Joan. As the plane passed directly above the village, she glimpsed how the hundreds of tiny dots clustered together in the car park.

If the plane had been able to fly any lower, she might have seen a limping William handing out bottles of free water and directing those separated from loved ones to a central meeting point. Might have seen Alice lean in through the open window of a farm truck to kiss the be-jangled driver, before running round to take the passenger seat beside her. But by now there was just a vast ocean passing below.

Mary leant back in her seat, ruminating on her panic-stricken decision to return the ring. The moment she understood the cosmic retribution she had unleashed, her one thought had been to rid herself of it. It might have meant their only option was a one-way flight, but at least her standing in the eyes of God could in time be rectified.

So the decision had made itself. They were going home. To farm. To raise their daughter. And serve their community. Their hand-to-mouth lives would resume, and in all likelihood they might never really know, in the checks and balances of life, how much had been lost and what if anything had been gained by their bid for something more.

As the plane slipped ever onwards over the face of the earth towards those she loved, she closed her eyes and said goodbye to the godless people. To dear Joe and Lola. To her hopes of ever finding streets paved with gold. And as Rene slept beside her, she bowed her head and prayed with a fervour so fierce, tears prickled like thorns beneath her closed lids.

Lord, shelter us through storm and earthquake, flood and fire. Now and forever more. Amen.

Rebecca Frayn is a critically acclaimed novelist, screenwriter, filmmaker and environmental activist. Her screenplay *The Lady*, which tells the story of Aung San Suu Kyi, was awarded the International Human Rights Film Award with Amnesty International. She also originated and wrote *Misbehaviour*, starring Kiera Knightley, which was released in every UK cinema to rave reviews. She has previously published two novels, *One Life* and *Deceptions*, and she is currently adapting *Lost in Ibiza* into a screenplay for the BFI. Rebecca is also working on Can Pep, a regenerative farm project in the north of Ibiza.

CAN CRISTOFOL

IBIZA

All profits from this book go to
Can Cristofol Finca Ecologica,
a regenerative farm in
the north of Ibiza.

@cancristofolibiza

With my most heartfelt thanks to the dear friends and family, together with the dedicated professionals, who have contributed along the way.